"So that went better than I expected," he said quietly, mirroring her own thoughts.

"Yeah, it was touch and go there for a while." Monica smiled at him, but when he returned it with a wicked grin of his own, the corner of her lip trembled. Really, the man's mouth should come with its own warning. *Caution: smirking leads to increased knee weakening.*

"Girls like me and Trina would rather have a new book than a pair of earrings any day."

"Yeah, you guys remind me of each other in a lot of ways."

Oh, jeez, did he just compare her to his almost eleven-year-old daughter?

"Like how?"

"Well, you guys are both kinda quiet and shy, but incredibly smart. Like I know there's got to be so much stuff going on in your brain, but for the life of me, I can't figure out what you're thinking. Still, I find myself wanting to know everything about you." He lifted up his sunglasses as he cast a glance across the cab of the truck and Monica squirmed in the passenger seat. "I want to know what makes you happy, what makes you sad, what makes you tick..."

* * *

AMERICAN HEROES:
They're coming home—and finding love!

Dear Reader,

My youngest sibling was born right before my senior year in high school—when I already had one foot out the door and was about to start the next chapter in my life. While we've always loved each other and spent time together, he and I have never really lived together...until now.

My brother recently moved in while finishing his master's program and, initially, I thought to myself, there's no way this single and social millennial is going to want to live with his middle-aged, bossy sister and her chaotic and sometimes annoying family. It'll be too much for everyone to handle. Yet, for some reason, when extra love shows up on your doorstep, there's always room to accommodate it.

The hero and heroine of my latest story are going to have to learn all about that type of accommodation.

Now, you might've caught glimpses of Ethan Renault and Monica Alvarez in my previous Sugar Falls books. What many of you might not have known was that behind the scenes there was some serious flirting and some potential relationship building going on when none of the townspeople were looking. Unfortunately, all of that changes when the SEAL's secret daughter arrives in Sugar Falls.

For more information on my other Special Edition books, visit my website at christyjeffries.com or chat with me on Twitter, @christyjeffries. You can also find me on Facebook and Instagram. I'd love to hear from you.

Enjoy,

Christy Jeffries

Facebook.com/AuthorChristyJeffries

Twitter.com/ChristyJeffries (@ChristyJeffries)

Instagram.com/Christy_Jeffries

The SEAL's
Secret Daughter

———

Christy Jeffries

Recycling programs
for this product may
not exist in your area.

ISBN-13: 978-1-335-57373-5

The SEAL's Secret Daughter

Copyright © 2019 by Christy Jeffries

Printed in U.S.A.

Christy Jeffries graduated from the University of California, Irvine, with a degree in criminology, and received her Juris Doctor from California Western School of Law. But drafting court documents and working in law enforcement was merely an apprenticeship for her current career in the dynamic field of mommyhood and romance writing. She lives in Southern California with her patient husband, two energetic sons and one sassy grandmother. Follow her online at christyjeffries.com.

Books by Christy Jeffries

Harlequin Special Edition

Sugar Falls, Idaho

A Marine for His Mom
Waking Up Wed
From Dare to Due Date
The Matchmaking Twins
The Makeover Prescription
A Family Under the Stars
The Firefighter's Christmas Reunion

American Heroes

A Proposal for the Officer

Montana Mavericks

The Maverick's Bridal Bargain

Montana Mavericks: The Lonelyhearts Ranch

The Maverick's Christmas to Remember

Visit the Author Profile page at Harlequin.com.

It had been six months since Ethan had officially left the United States Navy and landed in the small town of Sugar Falls, Idaho, to restart his life. Yet, except for the gourmet coffee maker sitting on the counter, the tiny kitchen in the apartment he'd rented above a downtown storefront was still just as sparse as the day he'd moved in.

The place had come furnished with only the basics and every once in a while, Ethan might pick up a few things at the market to add to the fridge. But it wasn't as though he enjoyed many meals at home. For some recovering alcoholics, socializing and eating at local restaurants with full-service bars might prove to be too much of a temptation. With Ethan, though, dining out provided him with more accountability—more eyes watching to keep him in line.

Besides, when he was alone, he had too much time to think.

As the coffee brewed, he made his way back to the bathroom and cranked the shower faucet to the highest setting. He was barely under the steaming spray long enough to get wet when he heard a pounding knock.

It wasn't even 0700 yet, so the chances of someone paying him a social call this early were pretty slim. *They probably have the wrong apartment*, he thought as he washed the shampoo from his hair. Yet, the knocking continued. Ethan debated staying in the shower and just ignoring whomever was banging on his front door. But what if it was a neighbor who needed a favor? Or a friend from one of his meetings who needed some encouragement?

Stepping out on the cold tile floor, he grabbed a towel and made his way toward the hall as he dried himself.

"Hold on a sec!" he yelled, crossing to his bedroom and grabbing a pair of jeans off the top of his dresser. The knocking paused briefly, but resumed before he could get his fly buttoned. Geez, what was this person's major emergency?

He tugged one of the thermal shirts off the hanger so quickly, the plastic triangle flew off the nearly empty closet rod. Ethan barely had his arms shoved through the sleeves when he finally yanked open the front door.

A woman he didn't recognize stood outside on the narrow landing, a lit cigarette hanging from the tight, thin line that was her mouth. She flicked the cigarette over the railing, not bothering to see where it landed below, and exhaled a cloud of smoke. "Ethan Renault?"

"Can I help you?" he replied without confirming his identity.

"You the same Ethan Renault who went to Sam Houston High?"

He narrowed his gaze, studying the woman before him. There were dark circles under her eyes and a permanent crease between her brows, as though she wore a constant frown. Had he gone to school with her?

When he didn't immediately respond, she continued. "Yep, it's you all right. Your hair might be shorter, but you still do that twitching thing with your fingers that makes you look like you're about to run off at the drop of a hat."

Ethan shoved his hands in his pockets and rocked forward on the balls of his bare feet. "Do I know you?"

The woman gave a snort, as though she expected quite a different response when she showed up unannounced on a stranger's doorstep this early in the middle of February. But Ethan patiently waited her out.

It was then that he noticed someone else standing on the stairs behind her. A young girl with dark, tangled hair holding a plastic grocery store bag kept her head down, fixated at the hole on her canvas sneaker where her big toe was popping through.

"I'm Chantal DeVecchio," the woman finally said, her added eye roll conveying her annoyance at not having been recognized right away. "And this," she said, gesturing to the girl, "is your daughter, Trina."

"But I don't have a daughter," Ethan told the woman who no longer looked anything like the eighteen-year-old cheerleader he'd once taken to the prom. His chest felt as though it was caving inward and he had to straighten his back and brace a hand against the door frame.

"She's yours," Chantal said. "And it's about time you man up and take care of your responsibilities."

Ethan's spine stiffened even more at the insult to his masculinity and the implication of his negligence. His eyes darted between his former high school girlfriend and the dark-haired child who appeared to only be interested in the patterns her sneakers made on the snow-covered steps. While he didn't know much about raising kids, he at least knew better than to let them go running around without socks when it was only twenty degrees outside.

"Why didn't you call me?" What he really wanted to ask was why had Chantal waited almost twelve years to spring such a life-changing surprise on him. "Or tell me before now?"

One minute, he'd been getting ready to head out for his regular breakfast over at the Cowgirl Up Café, wondering if today would be the day he'd finally convinced the shy server who waited on him every morning to go out on a date. The next minute, someone was banging on his front door and then accusing him of being a deadbeat dad to a child he'd never even known about.

"Because I didn't find out I was pregnant until after you'd joined the Navy and shipped out. It wasn't like you left a forwarding address before you and your dad ran out of town that summer."

It was true, Ethan had enlisted right after graduation. His dad was in the oil rigging business, constantly on the move to different cities depending on the latest job. Ethan had already switched high schools five times in three years and, that summer, the only new start he'd been eager to make was the change that would finally begin his adult life.

Scanning the alley behind the row of Victorian buildings that made up the downtown business district of Sugar Falls, Ethan realized that the local merchants would soon be filling up those parking spaces. "Maybe you should come inside and we can talk about this."

"Nothing to talk about," Chantal said, snatching the plastic sack out of her—and possibly his—daughter's hand and tossing it into his entryway. A purple T-shirt spilled out and landed on his bare foot. "I can't do this anymore. I'm just not cut out for motherhood. It's your turn to step up and be a father."

She turned around and gave Trina's shoulder an awkward hug. "I'm sorry, Trina," she said, a hint of sadness creeping into her voice. "But it's for the best. You'll see."

Chantal then brushed past the girl and marched down the steps. Ethan took a few strides to chase after the woman, but only made it halfway down the staircase when he realized that the child wasn't following. Or begging her mom not to leave her. The poor thing just stood there, looking as miserable as Ethan felt.

Something was ricocheting in his chest with a thumping urgency, but his body remained perfectly still. He needed to do something, to say something, but all he could do was grip the wrought iron handrail until his brain and his body could work in sync.

What he wouldn't give for a shot of bourbon right about now. Or for a call from his AA sponsor. But no amount of booze or platitudes or even SEAL team combat training could've prepared Ethan for the blow he'd just been dealt.

Not knowing what to do, his feet grew restless and the snow squishing between his toes began to sting, causing him to take a step toward the girl. Then he froze up all over again, like that time in Kabul when he and his buddy Boscoe faced an unexpected rainstorm of firepower. One wrong move could cause everything to blow up in his face. Worse than it already had.

An engine turned over in the alley below his apartment and he looked over his shoulder in time to see Chantal speeding off in a Geo Storm that might've been yellow twenty years ago. The shredded end of a rope holding the hatchback down to the bumper dragged along the wet asphalt as she made her escape.

A shiver started between Ethan's shoulder blades and traveled its way down his back. He ran a hand through his still damp hair and faced the young girl huddled on his porch.

His gut was telling him that it couldn't be possible for him to have a daughter. However, in the right light, if the child would look up and shove some of the stringy, black hair from her eyes, Ethan might concede that she somewhat resembled his French grandmother.

To be fair to Chantal, he had to admit he hadn't exactly kept track of every person he'd ever slept with over the years, but certainly he would've remembered if he'd gotten someone pregnant. Wouldn't he?

The girl made a sniffing sound, as though her nose was running, but she still didn't raise her head or look in his direction.

Shame flooded through him at the realization that he'd never even thought to ask her if she was okay. Or to try and put the child at ease. He opened his mouth to say something but couldn't command his tongue to form any words and ended up snapping it closed again. Damn. He was already proving himself to be a crappy father.

Clearing his throat, he reminded himself that he was once a member of an elite Special Forces team and had encountered dangers far graver than an eleven-year-old landing on his doorstep. "Hi," he said. "I'm Ethan."

"I know," the girl whispered, then wrapped a scrawny arm around her waist. It was then that he noticed she wasn't even wearing a sweater, let alone a coat.

"Why don't you come inside, Trina? It's freezing out here."

The girl eventually lifted her face and his lungs seized. Her eyes weren't wide with fear, as Ethan would've expected. Nor were they filled with humiliation or hurt, which would've been understandable given the way her mother had just dumped her here. Instead, they were completely without expression. Witnessing their empty depths would've been downright spooky if he hadn't recognized that same look in his own eyes the night after his last covert ops assignment. Or recognized the identical sapphire-blue color that ran rampant in the Renault family.

Trina didn't decline his invitation, but she wasn't exactly quick to make a decision either. She had to be equally as afraid of him as he was of her. Stranger danger and all that. She must've heard her mother announce that he was her father, but that didn't mean she necessarily believed it. Well, that made two of them.

Being careful not to touch her as he stepped around her shivering form, Ethan held open the door, hoping that the heat coming from his apartment would be more inviting than the ugly used furniture inside. He was about to go into the kitchen and grab his cell phone to call for backup when finally, with an apprehensive look cast in Ethan's direction, her feet shuffled toward him.

Trina gave him a measured glance before swooping low to grab her purple T-shirt and shoving it back into her grocery bag. She held the recovered belongings close to her chest, as though they were some sort of shield that could protect her from him.

"Are you hungry?" Ethan asked. He left the front door wide-open as he walked toward the kitchen, not wanting her to feel trapped. Would she follow? Or would she run off, just as her mother had?

"Kinda," Trina replied, her voice again no louder than a whisper. She was on the thin side and he wondered when she'd had her last meal.

Ethan stared at his bare counters, knowing full well the only thing he could offer the girl right now would be a mug of triple-brewed dark roast.

"I…uh…wasn't exactly expecting company." He shoved his hands in his pockets and rocked back on his heels. "I usually eat breakfast at the café across the street."

Trina tilted her head at him, her blue eyes still empty, her arms still clutched tightly to her in apprehension. If she was truly his daughter, Ethan wanted to do the right thing by her. He just wasn't convinced that taking care of her all by himself would be the right thing.

He really could use some direction here. This town was

bursting with know-it-all busybodies who had opinions on everything from which colors to paint the historical homes to who should play point guard for the high school basketball team. Unfortunately, none of those people were currently inside his apartment.

"I've got an idea," Ethan said, but Trina's blank expression didn't waver. "I'm going to grab my coat and, uh, something for you to put on to keep warm, and we'll go across the street and grab a hot breakfast."

Surely someone over at the Cowgirl Up Café would have an idea of what he should do with the girl.

"I'll be right back," he said, walking down the hallway toward his bedroom. As he looked at the few clothes hanging in his closet, he wondered if Trina would still be standing in his living room when he came out. Or had she already made a run for it the second he turned his back? It was what he would've done in her situation.

But she was right where he'd left her when he returned with a fleece-lined hooded sweatshirt branded with the eagle and trident logo. "Here, this is the best I could come up with. But we're not going very far."

She had to drop her bag on the scuffed dining room table to take the sweatshirt from him. He sat at one of the cheap pine chairs to pull on his work boots, trying not to notice the way Trina kept having to push the sleeves up her arms to keep her hands from getting drowned by the heavy material of the borrowed sweatshirt.

Locking the front door behind him, Ethan realized that Trina was very careful not to get in front of him. She would only follow after he'd already passed. Whenever his team had infiltrated compounds and taken captives or brought in noncombatants for questioning, they'd been trained to always stay behind the enemy—to never turn their backs on a potential threat.

The thought that his own daughter might view him as a threat made his stomach go sour, however, Ethan didn't say anything as they walked down the steps to the alley and then through the narrow walkway that put them out on to Snowflake Boulevard. When they got on the main street of town, he glanced down the block toward the new public safety building that housed both the police department and the fire station. It would be so easy to lead Trina over there and drop her off. His mind calculated how long it would take him to leave her at the entrance and then hop into his secondhand truck and drive down the mountain to the Boise airport.

How long would it take to leave this whole mess behind him?

But he'd lived his life being on the move, alternating between taking on the most dangerous assignments to come through his unit and then drowning himself in a bottle to escape the unpleasantness of the world. The whole point of his leaving the Navy and relocating to Sugar Falls was so he could finally slow down, sober up and figure out what his next chapter would be.

He just hadn't expected fatherhood to be on the first page.

Monica Alvarez was balancing a tray of refilled salt and pepper shakers in one hand and a pot of decaf in the other when the tingling bell sounded above the saloon-style front doors of the Cowgirl Up Café. As a part-time waitress, early Wednesday mornings were usually her easiest shifts—most of the weekend tourists were long gone, replaced with only a handful of regulars lounging in their favorite booths, ordering their usuals, which she now had memorized. However, it wasn't the blast of frigid air coming in from outside that made the welcoming smile fade from Monica's lips.

It wasn't even the arrival of the hunky contractor who ordered the same exact breakfast—four scrambled egg whites, turkey sausage patties, sliced tomatoes and black coffee with a side of flirtatious banter—that made her pause. It was the unexpected appearance of a young girl cowering behind him that had stopped Monica in her tracks and caused the ceramic cowboy boot–shaped spice shakers on her tray to wobble.

The first time she'd waited on Ethan Renault several months ago, she'd written him off as a harmless bad boy who would eventually give up once he figured out that she wasn't interested in his type. Initially, it had been easy to brush off the sexy smirk and ignore the lazy way his thick-lashed eyes followed her as she messed up orders and proved herself to be an incompetent waitress.

But the man had been patient and stealthy and, occasionally, he'd even made her laugh. Last week, when she'd been at her real job, Ethan had come into the library and asked for a recommendation. Anyone who knew her understood that the best way to get Monica involved in a conversation was to talk about books. That's how she related best to people, by understanding them as readers firsts. Knowing a person's reading habits revealed so much, it was like a secret superpower that only librarians and booksellers possessed.

She'd given him a copy of *Rejection for Dummies* and he'd happily taken it without batting his handsome blue eyes. Then, the first thing he'd told her Monday morning was that the book was okay, but that he was waiting for

the movie. While Monica hadn't had the time—or the desire—to date much since college, she'd had a feeling that
his line was a lead-in and that Ethan would've asked her
out to the movies if a very confused and agitated Gran
hadn't called the restaurant right then and needed Monica
to come home to help find the cat that they didn't own.

Today, she'd been expecting him to pick up the flirtatious banter right where he'd left off and she'd even toyed
around with the idea of accepting his offer—if he asked
her out, anyway—because she could barely remember the
last time she'd gotten out and had a little fun for herself.

However, there was nothing jovial or flirty about the
man right this second. In fact, the deep grooves along his
brow and the hardened line of his jaw made him look like
a completely different person—like he'd been hiding his
true personality all along.

With only two other occupied booths in the restaurant
this early in the morning, there were half a dozen sets
of eyes trained on the new arrivals. The curious stares
coupled with the silence spoke volumes and reassured
Monica that she wasn't the only one who'd noticed that
something was out of the ordinary.

A prickling sensation made its way down the back
of her neck and she cleared her throat. "Table for two?"

"Uh…yeah," he finally said, and glanced behind him
at the girl. Ethan normally walked into the restaurant
with a grin and a sense of purpose, saying hello to all the
locals before grabbing his favorite seat at the end of the
counter. Today, though, he didn't make a move toward
his usual spot despite the fact it was empty. He didn't really move at all.

"How about that table over there." Monica used her
chin to nod toward an empty corner booth that was on

the opposite side of where the other diners were now blatantly staring at them.

"Great," Ethan replied, and began walking in that direction. He took a few steps, then paused and turned to the child. "Is this okay?"

The girl's only response was to follow behind him, her head not lifting. Something about the child tugged at Monica's heart and reminded her of how shy and awkward she'd once been at that same age.

Monica took the tray of shakers to the prep station and switched out the pot of decaf for regular coffee, since Ethan normally drank at least three cups.

When she returned to their table, she passed them both laminated menus. Not that Ethan ever needed one, but something was definitely off about him this morning and she no longer knew what to expect. Using the same smile she used during the tiny tots reading circle at the library, she faced the girl and said, "Hi. I'm Monica."

The child lifted her face and Monica gasped at the resemblance to Ethan. Their mouths were the same shape and their chins shared matching dimples. If the girl's stringy hair was washed and brushed, it would likely be the exact inky-black shade as Ethan's, as well. Yet, it was the bottomless sapphire-blue eyes that were the dead giveaway.

They were definitely related.

That didn't make sense, though. Monica could've sworn that she'd once overheard him bragging about being single and carefree. Plus, she was positive that he'd told Freckles, the owner of the café, that his mom died when he was a boy and his father had passed away a few years ago and he didn't have any other family.

So then where had this child come from?

If Freckles hadn't taken the morning off, the nosy older woman would've been asking all kinds of questions, like whether this was the girl's first time in Sugar Falls and how long was she visiting. Unfortunately, Monica wasn't quite as smooth when it came to starting conversations with the customers. Sure, she liked listening to people talk and picking up information here and there, but she didn't have that ability of asking the right kinds of questions to illicit much more than a two- or three-word response. Unless it was about their favorite books.

But a million questions were floating through her head as she stared at the child, who was having trouble keeping her hands pushed through the sleeves of the man-size sweatshirt she'd obviously borrowed from Ethan.

There was still snow outside this time of year. Where was the girl's jacket?

Monica turned over Ethan's mug and poured him a steaming cup of coffee, but he avoided eye contact so she couldn't read any clues on his normally friendly face. Turning to the girl, she said, "It's pretty cold this morning. How about some hot chocolate?"

The girl's eyes grew wide, and for an instant, an almost…craving expression flashed across her face, as though she'd never wanted anything more. Yet, her only reply was to study Ethan with a guarded look.

"Do you like hot chocolate?" Ethan asked her, and the girl nodded slowly. "Then hot chocolate it is." He turned to Monica. "This is Trina. We're still…uh…getting to know each other."

A chill spread through Monica, making her skin prickle with unease. Stumbling backward, she retreated to the prep station behind the counter. She fumbled with the bottle of chocolate sauce several times as she thought about Ethan's odd response. How did he not know the girl before now? They were clearly related.

Monica caught a movement out of the corner of her eye and turned just in time to see Trina dart into the hallway leading toward the restrooms. A hissing sound, followed by a blast of steam, drew her attention back to the complex frothing machine her boss had installed a few weeks ago and she barely got the thing shut off in time to prevent the hot milk from splattering everywhere. Monica cupped the warm mug in her trembling hands as she quickly walked to the table where Ethan was now sitting alone.

She needed to hurry if she wanted to talk to him before Trina returned from the restroom. Out of all the questions she wanted answered, the first one that came tumbling out of her mouth was, "Is she yours?"

Monica winced at her own words, her whisper-soft tone not making the personal question sound any less rude.

But Ethan either hadn't been bothered or he was too absorbed in his own thoughts to notice the impolite tone. He shrugged his shoulders, the expression on his face almost trancelike. "That's what her mother said when she left her on my front porch this morning."

"What do you mean, her mother left her on your front porch?" Monica had to brace her hand on the cowhide printed backrest of the booth. She was no longer whispering, drawing the curious stares from the other side of the restaurant.

"She knocked on my door this morning. I didn't even recognize her."

"Trina?" Disgust rose in Monica's throat. How had the man not recognized his own daughter?

"No. Her mom. I guess we dated in high school and..."

Ethan gave another shrug and it was all she could do not to grab two fistfuls of his plaid work shirt and shake the rounded muscles of his shoulders.

"You *guess*?" Monica swallowed a lump of annoyance. She wasn't only ticked off with his answer, she was angry with herself. Disappointed at how easily she'd been blinded by her building attraction to a man who didn't seem to know anything about his own daughter—including her existence. "So where is her mother now?"

"Her mother?" His brows formed a V and Monica rolled her eyes in frustration. She could handle Ethan easily enough when he was being a charming flirt, or even when he professed to be interested in her tongue-in-cheek book recommendations. However, if he was hoping this whole confused pretense would draw her sympathy, he was sorely mistaken.

"Yes. The person you dated back in high school? The mother of your child?"

"Right. Chantal drove off. She said she wasn't any good at being a mom and threw Trina's bag of clothes at me, telling me it was my turn to step up."

There was nothing more reprehensible than a man who didn't take care of his responsibilities. No amount of sex appeal or charm could make up for a lack of character. Her own father had been the same way and Monica shuddered at how close she'd come to falling under Ethan's spell.

At how close she'd come to repeating her own mother's same mistakes.

Chapter Two

Monica's growing revulsion was soon replaced with pity as Trina returned from the bathroom, her chin low and her face averted from the curious stares from the other customers as she carried a balled-up blue sweatshirt under one arm. Monica took in his daughter's lanky unwashed hair and the oversize T-shirt advertising Mesquite Muffler Mart and Automotive Repair. Not exactly a fashion staple in most preteen girls' closets.

The child's voice was low and gravelly when she whispered, "Why do they all keep looking over here?"

Monica glanced toward her Wednesday morning regulars. Scooter and Jonesy, the two older cowboys, were mostly harmless although a little gossipy at times. She couldn't say the same for the other three ladies, who apparently weren't in any hurry to leave, despite the fact they'd already paid their checks and had their own local businesses to open.

Monica had grown up in Sugar Falls and, as much as she withered under the curious stares and wagging tongues, at least she was used to the presence of the small-town busybodies. It had to be twenty times worse for a child who was also an outsider.

"You know what?" Monica stood up straighter. "The cook is out on a smoke break. Why don't you guys come on back to the kitchen and I'll fix your breakfast myself? It's much more private back there."

She was still holding the mug of hot chocolate and tried to give Trina a reassuring smile before leading the way toward the swinging door. It took a few seconds before the girl followed, and Monica pulled out the single wooden stool near a stainless steel counter for Trina, not bothering with a thought for where Ethan would sit.

He could either plop himself on the ground or go on and slither out the front door for all she cared. Instead, she had to hold back every insulting word on the tip of her tongue when Ethan finally wormed his way back into the kitchen. After all, it wouldn't be fair to say anything that might upset Trina, the poor little girl who'd just been abandoned by her own mother.

Monica added a heavy dollop of whipped cream to the mug of cocoa and handed it to the waif of a child. "Careful, it's hot."

Ethan must've left his own coffee back at the table and Monica couldn't help but shoot daggers at the man who stood by the door, his hands buried in his jean pockets and his eyes darting around nervously, as though he was also plotting his own escape. As though leaving a child behind was no different than abandoning his cup of coffee.

A knot of concern wedged between her rib cage. Monica had also grown up without a father, but at least she'd had Gran. Trina, on the other hand, didn't seem to have anyone. Maybe someone should call child protective services or even the police department and file some sort of report. She made a mental note to do some research on it. Once she got Trina fed.

"Would you like blueberries in your pancakes?" Monica asked.

Trina shot a questioning glance to her father. Or at least the man who'd sired her. "Does that cost extra?"

"I…uh…" Ethan's normally cocky voice stuttered and Monica would've laughed at how many notches his ego must've been taken down if the circumstances hadn't come at Trina's expense. He moved closer and leaned a hip against the basin of the prep sink. "You can get whatever you want. Don't worry about the cost."

The girl let out a breath and put an elbow onto the counter, resting her chin on her palm as she studied the man. Monica poured some batter onto the griddle and threw in a scoop of blueberries, constantly glancing back over her shoulder to watch the silent staring contest between father and daughter.

"Only rich people say things like 'don't worry about the cost,'" Trina said, and Monica choked back a giggle. She was glad to see that the child was finally finding her voice and speaking up. "Are you one of those guys who lives in a crappy apartment, but you're really a secret billionaire?"

"I'm not rich. And my apartment isn't *that* crappy. I mean it's not really decorated or anything because I've only lived there a few months. And I wasn't exactly expecting company."

"Ethan," Monica warned, unsure of the direction that this conversation was taking and not wanting the man to do any further damage than he'd already done by being an absent father for the past however many years. "How old are you, Trina?"

"Eleven."

"Wow." Ethan exhaled a long, slow hiss of air. "I didn't... I don't... I... Wow. I've never been in this situation before."

"It's fine if you don't want me," Trina said when Ethan apparently couldn't finish whatever it was he'd been trying to say. Whatever cheap apologies he might've offered for missing the first eleven years of her life. "I have a caseworker back in Galveston. If you call her, she'll get me a bus ticket or an emergency foster home or something."

"Have you been in foster care before?" Ethan asked, inching closer, and Monica held her breath, praying the young girl had somehow had a happy and fulfilling life up until now.

"Every year or so, my mother decides that she can't deal with me or with life and takes off somewhere. I used to live with my grandmother, but Gran died a few months ago."

"Oh," was all Ethan could say, and Monica clenched the spatula tighter, her heart clenching at the girl's casual indifference about her situation.

"I have a Gran, too," Monica offered, sliding a very uneven pancake onto a plate. Cooking wasn't exactly her forte, but neither was waitressing. "She also raised me after my father left."

Trina smiled and mumbled a "Thanks." But Monica wasn't sure if it was for the attempt at making her breakfast or for the attempt at understanding her situation. Or both.

Ethan must've heard something he didn't like, though, because he scrunched up his nose and attempted a subtle head shake at Monica. Perhaps he didn't appreciate someone pointing out the obvious comparison to another deadbeat dad, but he couldn't very well deny that he'd also left his daughter. Well, Monica supposed he *could* deny knowing about her in the first place, but he apparently knew better than to discuss all of his excuses right in front of the poor girl.

Monica set the dish in front of Trina and said, "Eat up and then we'll figure out who we need to call."

"Why would we need to call anyone?" Ethan asked. "And can I get one of those pancakes?"

"No, you may not." Monica squared her shoulders and turned toward him. Stepping behind Trina, who was drowning her plate in syrup, Monica jerked her thumb at the area in the corner where Freckles kept the stacks of flour and the cans of shortening for her famous biscuits. Walking that way, she had to wave an arm at Ethan who was slow to get the hint.

It was a tighter spot than she'd anticipated, and when he wedged his muscular six-foot frame in next to her, she was hit with the lemony scent of his shampoo. His face was only inches from hers and she lowered her gaze to the soft flannel of his work shirt and the way it stretched across his broad chest.

To get her mind off his physical nearness, Monica curled her fingers into her palms, squeezing until her nails dug into her hands. Finally, she was able to lift her head and unclench her jaw long enough to whisper, "What do you mean 'why would we need to call anyone?'"

"If she's my daughter, then she's not going back to some social worker in Galveston."

If she's his daughter? It didn't take a paternity test to prove the two looked exactly alike, including those haunted blue eyes.

"Lower your voice," she admonished, squinting past him to see if Trina had overheard. "She isn't a lost puppy. You can't just take a child home and keep her."

"Why not?" he asked, and her frustration mounted, heating her face. Or maybe it was the way his bicep brushed against her shoulder when he shoved his hands into his jean pockets.

She didn't have a legal argument, or at least she wouldn't until her shift was over and she went to the library and did some research. So Monica attempted to argue using common sense. "Because she doesn't know you, Ethan. She's got to be terrified."

"And sending her off with some stranger to a foster home wouldn't be even scarier?"

"I can hear you, you know," Trina called out, not bothering to turn around.

Monica pursed her lips and shot Ethan a pointed look of annoyance since she couldn't very well say, *Now look what you did.*

"Sorry, Trina." Ethan returned to where his daughter was seated.

Monica held her breath. She really should be back in the dining room, checking on her customers. But her heart was tearing apart at the way the girl just shrugged everything off, no longer making eye contact with the man who'd fathered her.

"I'm normally not so rude," he offered, and Monica had to give him that. In fact, Ethan was usually quite a smooth talker. Too smooth, if you asked her. "But seeing you, finding out...well, I've just been caught off guard."

Just then, Scooter Deets, one of the old-timers who ate at the café every morning, sauntered by the pass-through window and held up a hot pink coffee mug. Scooter had checked out a book on plumbing two years ago and his overdue fine was pushing triple digits. "Don't mind me, y'all. I'm just grabbing myself a refill."

Trying to fill up on gossip was more like it, Monica thought.

"I'll be right there," she said to the cowboy, who was normally hard of hearing unless there was something juicy going on. Monica turned to Trina. "Give me a couple of minutes and we'll put our heads together and figure something out."

"What's there to figure out? She's my daughter. She's coming home with me."

Monica pursed her lips and pointed to the corner of shelves so that Trina wouldn't have to listen to them talking about her. Again. This time, when he followed her, Monica steeled herself for his closeness. "What do you even know about raising a child, much less a daughter?"

"Like I said, I'm a bit out of sorts, so you'll have to forgive me for being rude," Ethan started, indicating that something rude was about to come out of his normally smirking mouth. "But it really isn't your business."

The insult hit its mark and Monica's aggravated groan sounded more like a defensive gasp. "You're right, Ethan Renault. You're not my business at all, thank God. However, someone needs to be looking out for what's best for Trina and you obviously haven't shown an interest in doing so in the past."

"I didn't even know she existed before this morning," he hissed. "So how could I have shown *anything* in the past?"

"Psfhh." Monica's hands went to her hips. "The fact that you didn't know in the first place is telling enough."

"I was in high school the last time I saw her mom. I was just a dumb kid back then. How would you like someone to judge you for what you did when you were a teenager?"

The breath caught in Monica's throat. When she'd been that age, she'd been working two jobs and studying around the clock to keep her grades high enough to win a college scholarship. She was more likely to be judged for being a boring stick-in-the-mud.

The squeaking hinge of the kitchen's back door sounded and Monica looked up, expecting to see the cook returning from his break. Instead, she saw nobody. When she glanced over to where Trina was sitting, the only thing left was an empty plate.

"Oh hell," Ethan said, running a hand through his short hair and sprinting toward the door.

The flash of panic had been evident on his face and Monica suddenly regretted every accusation she'd just thrown his way. She'd been reliving all of her old painful memories of her own father and projecting those past hurts onto an easy target.

She followed Ethan to the back door, but before she could exit, he came barreling back inside. "She's not in the alley."

"Where do you think she could've gone?" Monica gnawed on her lower lip.

"I have no idea. I really don't know anything about her. When she showed up on my doorstep an hour ago, she looked cold and hungry. I didn't have anything for her to eat so that's why we came here. I was hoping to get some answers, but now she's disappeared."

A tinkling bell sounded over the front door and Monica wanted to stomp her foot in frustration. Now wasn't the time for more customers to show up.

"Maybe she went back to your place?" Monica suggested. Every fiber in her body wanted to chase after the poor girl and keep her safe, but she couldn't until the second waitress came on duty for her shift. "You go look for her there and I'll stay here in case she comes back."

"It took me eleven years to find her," Ethan said, his eyes pleading with Monica's as though she was the only one who could help him. "I don't want to lose her again."

"I have no clue where to even look for her," Ethan said to his boss over the phone's speaker as he slowly cruised his truck up and down Snowflake Boulevard, the center of the touristy Victorian downtown. Since he was expected at his contracting job at eight, it seemed only responsible to call his employer and confide in everything that had happened.

"Maybe you should call the police department," Kane Chatterson offered.

"I'm pretty sure I heard Monica Alvarez say she was going to call when I tore out of the Cowgirl Up half an hour ago. Hold on, my call waiting is beeping." Ethan looked at his screen and saw the number. His adrenaline, which had been pumping steadily until this point, suddenly nosedived. "It's the police. I'll call you back."

Switching over to the other line, Ethan didn't bother with pleasantries. "Carmen, did you find her?"

"Monica found her in the ladies' room at the Cowgirl Up," Officer Carmen Gregson replied, and Ethan's exhale came out in a whoosh. "Apparently, she circled back and went in the front door, but Monica didn't have your cell number. I'm heading over there now, but we might want to go somewhere a little less gossipy than the local diner so we can get this worked out."

The fear clenching around his gut lessened, yet Ethan's pulse remained elevated with apprehension. And confusion. Two hours ago, he didn't even know he had a daughter, didn't know his world could be so thrown off its axis before it got shaken up and thrown again.

Ethan eased his truck off the road and scrubbed at the lower half of his face, the face he hadn't had time to shave this morning. More air released from his lungs before he asked, "What do we need to work out?"

"Just a heads-up, Renault…" The police officer, his best friend's wife, was also former military and it put Ethan more at ease to have someone use his last name. "When Monica called it in, she said the girl mentioned something about a caseworker back in Texas. That means, by law, I'm required to notify them or the local child protective services."

"Will they take her from me?" Ethan hadn't exactly been doing cartwheels at the opportunity to be a father, but there was a ball of nausea welling up in his belly at the thought of his child—someone who shared his blood— being raised by a complete stranger.

"Why don't you meet me at the café and we can walk the girl over to the station or someplace else where we can talk."

"Right," Ethan said, returning his foot to the accelerator and steering back onto the road. "I'm on my way."

Thankfully, his first instinct wasn't to stop by the bar or the liquor store before he got there—not that either would be open this early. Still, it was a relief that his steady hands now offered his mixed-up mind some focus.

Ethan again toyed with the idea of calling his sponsor to tell him about this recent development, but he didn't quite know what was going on, let alone know how to explain it. The best thing he could do was talk to Trina and the authorities and figure out his next step.

By the time he found a parking spot on the street between the Cowgirl Up Café and his apartment, Officer Gregson and Monica were already walking his way. His daughter appeared even more fragile between the two adult females, her head down and her face hidden behind a mess of stringy, limp hair.

He'd heard about dads who fell in love with their newborns right there in the delivery room. Something must be wrong with Ethan then, because he hadn't experienced an instant bond with the girl when he'd first seen her outside his door this morning. In fact, she'd been a sullen, quiet little thing who would barely look at him—not that he could blame her. But now, desperation pricked at his skin as Trina approached and he needed some sort of sign that she was okay. Or at least, that she *would* be okay.

Carmen must've taken pity on Ethan's panicked expression because she told him, "The three of us had a good talk in the ladies' room and we all agreed that everyone would feel more comfortable talking at your place so we can get a better handle on the situation."

Ethan definitely didn't have a handle on any of this and it had to be obvious. Worse, they'd most likely overwhelmed the poor girl when he and Monica stood there arguing about his inability to raise a child right in front of her, essentially driving her away. While Monica's earlier accusations still rankled at him, now wasn't the time to continue that discussion.

As the trio of females silently trudged up the stairs behind him, Ethan unlocked his front door for more visitors than his apartment had ever held at one time. At least in the few months that he'd lived there.

"I need to use the bathroom," Trina mumbled as she walked past him and toward his hallway. His first instinct was to ask the girl why she was always running to the restroom, however, it might be easier to talk with the others if he didn't have to watch his words. Plus, there wasn't a window in there so it wasn't like Trina could escape. Again.

"Is this everything she has?" Monica folded a denim pair of shorts that had fallen out of the plastic grocery bag Trina had left on the dining room table earlier. "There isn't much inside here."

"Any paperwork?" Carmen asked her, and Ethan had to bite his tongue to keep from asking why Monica was even a part of this. "It would help if we had an official name or something to go by before I call any other agencies."

For such a seemingly shy and reserved woman, Monica certainly had no problem barging into his personal life and offering up her opinions. Although, Trina had definitely opened up more when the quiet librarian and part-time waitress had spoken to her. He wondered what else she and his daughter had discussed in that ladies' room while Ethan had been tearing through town in a full panic.

"Here," Monica said, holding up a pink-and-blue document titled Birth Certificate. Despite the lenses of her glasses, he could still see the hint of accusation in the woman's brown eyes as she focused on Ethan, her forehead lifted in a questioning crease. "Your name is listed under *Father*."

What had Ethan done wrong? He'd always used protection, even back then, never relying on someone else's methods of birth control. Yet, Monica was frowning at him as though he'd gotten *her* pregnant. As if her sleeping with him would ever be a possibility now.

Her rich, dark brown hair was piled up into its usual messy ponytail of curls and he preferred her in the snug, turquoise T-shirt all the waitresses at the café sported rather than in the monotone cardigan sweaters she usually wore at the library. Ethan thought Monica had been warming up to him the past month—she'd even begun to smile at him on the mornings she'd pulled extra shifts at the Cowgirl Up. She had a cute little dimple in the side of one cheek and each time he'd caught a flash of it, Ethan felt as though someone had given him a key to Heaven.

He'd be lying if he said he hadn't already given plenty of thought to what it would be like to get her out of her clothes completely, to be able to kiss every bit of her light amber skin and hopefully be the one to make her smile, over and over. Judging by her current glare, though, he doubted that he'd ever see that dimple again, let alone find out what was underneath that T-shirt. Maybe he'd dodged a bullet by not asking her out, after all.

"Let me see that." Carmen took the certificate before studying it. "Yep, your name is definitely on it."

Ethan walked over to Carmen and scanned the paper over her shoulder. "Trina DeVecchio Renault." She even had his last name.

"Date of birth, February 8." Eleven years ago. He didn't have to do much calculating to know the timing was right. Confusion made the corners of his lips turn down. "But I never signed anything. And my birth date on it is wrong. Hell, I didn't even know about the girl until today."

"Well, someone signed off on it and that's all that matters." Carmen hooked her thumbs in her leather duty belt. "I would still need to run everything through the system to make sure the document is legitimate, but if it is, then the kinship law would apply here."

"I have no idea what that means," Ethan admitted, glancing at Monica to see if she was judging him even more for not knowing anything about family law.

"Technically," Carmen continued. "This Chantal De-Vecchio, assuming she had legal custody of the girl in the first place, gave you temporary guardianship as another family member when she left her in your care. Therefore, the state will recognize you as Trina's temporary guardian."

"Is there a note or a paper in there that says she was giving her to me?" Ethan asked, looking at the bag in Monica's hands.

"No, just two pictures." Monica held up a photograph of an older woman sitting on the front porch of a mobile home—Trina's grandmother, perhaps. The second photo was actually on shiny magazine paper and showed a basket full of calico kittens.

Even Ethan had more personal belongings and mementos when he'd shipped off to basic training.

"For whatever it's worth—" Monica gave a quick glance toward the hallway then lowered her voice to the whisper-soft tone she normally used inside the library "—when I spoke to her in the ladies' room, she admitted that she would rather stay with you than go into foster care."

"Then why did she run off?" Ethan tried to whisper back, but it sounded more like an angry hiss.

"Probably because she thought you didn't want her?"

Monica put her hands on her hips and, if Ethan had been in his right mind, he would've appreciated the way her defensive stance showed off her lush curves. He'd been trying to get this woman out of her shell for the past few months, yet now that she was finally directing some passion his way, the angry heat in her eyes caused him to take a step back.

"I'd suggest hiring an attorney and making everything legal," Carmen said, typing something into her smartphone. "But, in the meantime, depending on what the CPS records show, as long as Trina's not a ward of the court, I feel comfortable releasing her into your custody."

One advantage to living in a small town was that when people knew you, they didn't mind giving you the benefit of the doubt. Ethan finally understood the next step he would have to take.

Now, he just needed to convince a scared and abandoned little girl that he was her best option. Too bad he hadn't convinced himself yet.

Chapter Three

"But what if she changes her mind and doesn't want to stay with him?" Monica asked Carmen when the two women got downstairs and circled around to the sidewalk in front of Domino's Deli. "What if she runs away again?"

"Then I'd suggest you let Freckles know that the girl might show up at the Cowgirl Up again. Maybe she thinks of it as a safe space."

"Does that mean you think she might not feel safe with him?"

"I know you're worried about the girl." Carmen placed a reassuring hand on her shoulder. "I can't predict the future any better than you can, but I got the impression that she ran off the first time thinking she was saving face. You know, getting away before her father could reject her. Kids that age have a tendency to act tough when they're afraid. When we talked to her back in the restaurant and told her that Ethan was out searching for her and seemed genuinely worried about her well-being, she appeared willing to give him a chance. Listen, Monica, I never would've released her into his custody if I thought it wasn't in her best interest."

Monica had always liked and trusted the female police officer, who preferred mysteries while her twin sons raced through a couple of *Magic Tree House* books a week. They'd never really socialized much, but then again, Monica wasn't much for hanging out with her neighbors or attending the community activities.

She was too busy working two jobs and taking care of Gran. Being pleasant and making small talk with the customers at the restaurant took all the energy she had left. Still, she knew how to keep her eyes and ears open and Carmen Gregson was compassionate with the townspeople, observant on her patrols, and dedicated to her job and family. Everyone in town valued the woman's opinion.

Looking at her watch, Monica estimated that she had fifteen more minutes before she would have to leave for the library. So she didn't bother keeping the hesitation from her voice as she asked, "What do you think of Ethan Renault?"

"In what way?" Carmen was a cop and an observer. Like Monica, she probably did her research and analyzed things from all angles.

"As a father, I guess." Monica stated the obvious when what she really wanted to ask—what she'd really wanted to know for the past few months—was if she was a complete fool for having a teensy tiny crush on the man.

But her ill-advised attraction to Ethan was something she could barely acknowledge to herself. There was no way she would say it out loud. Besides, now certainly wasn't the time to ask about the guy's relationship suitability—which had lost all potential anyway the second Trina showed up.

Carmen turned to face her, seeming to look beyond Monica's forced casual expression and deep down into what her mind was really thinking. Wrapping an arm around her midsection, Monica toyed with the tie of her apron, trying not to feel too exposed.

"He's one of my husband's best friends, so keep in mind that my opinion might be a little biased."

Monica nodded. "Grain of salt taken."

"When I first met Ethan, I would've pegged him for a typical Navy SEAL with a cocky ego and an adrenaline complex. The type of guy who doesn't mind breaking hearts or breaking bones if it involves having a good time. Although, I'd also pegged Luke the same way and he proved me wrong. I think Ethan has been through a lot and seen a lot, yet doesn't talk about the darker stuff. Probably hides it behind that flirty smile and arrogant charm."

So Monica wasn't the only one who'd noticed the lazy, seductive grin. Or the possibility of a string of broken hearts left in his wake. Resolution made her spine stiffen and her commitment to not fall prey to his flirtatious banter intensified.

"But," Carmen continued, "I also think he takes his responsibilities seriously and he isn't afraid of a little adversity. Luke told me that of all his former teammates, Ethan was the one he trusted the most. I know the guy probably doesn't seem like the fatherly type now, but Trina is in safe hands."

Monica gave a slight nod as she exhaled, but she still held on to her doubts. Her own father had come and gone from her life many times before he'd finally left for good. She and her mom had lived with Gran until Monica was six, and when her mother passed, Gran seemed to think that her dad might come back to get her. Part of Monica had been terrified that she would have to leave her grandmother and the only home she'd ever known. But the other part of her had been excited that she could have her father back, that she might finally get to experience a dad's love. Just like Monica, Trina had to be nervous and terrified of what awaited her, but maybe she was just a little excited, too. Excited that she would now get a chance to know the man who made up part of her DNA.

Unfortunately, that excitement would soon fade once Ethan let the girl down. Even with Carmen's vote of confidence on keeping her safe, there was no way a tried-and-true bachelor like him could change his ways and provide a nurturing home to a preteen who'd just had her world turned upside down.

For Trina's sake, Monica would hope for the best. But leopards didn't change their spots. It was a good reminder for the next time she found herself attracted to a man like Ethan. Blowing a curl out of her face, she couldn't believe that she'd been secretly enjoying his flirtatious banter every Monday and Wednesday when she'd waited on him during her breakfast shift, hoping he'd ask her out.

A crackling sound shot out from the walkie-talkie on Carmen's duty belt and Monica recognized the dispatcher's voice through the static. A retiree with a tie-dye shirt and comb-over hairstyle that didn't fool anyone, Harv Jenkins preferred science fiction and the occasional graphic novel. In addition to being a part-time dispatcher, he also volunteered at the senior citizens center and had always been sweet to Gran, despite the fact that her grandmother hated his comic book drawing classes. But his words today made Monica's pulse leap. "Be advised, we

just got a call about the fire alarm going off at the Alvarez house again."

The siren from the nearby fire engine rang out and a
heavy ball of dread settled in Monica's stomach, a familiar feeling lately where her grandmother was concerned.

"You want me to drive you in the patrol car?" Carmen offered.

"No thanks." Monica jogged across the street toward
the Cowgirl Up Café and called over her shoulder, "As
long as it's not as bad as last time, I'm going to need my
own car to get to work after I check on her."

She'd already left her shift at the restaurant early to
help with Trina. Now she was going to be late to open the
library to help with Gran. And it was Western Wednesday, which meant that she only had thirty minutes before
the Louis L'Amour book club arrived for their monthly
meeting in the reading room.

At this rate, Monica was going to lose both of her jobs.
And then where would she and Gran be?

Trina came out of the bathroom as soon as Monica and
Carmen left. Ethan thought about offering to show her
around the small apartment, but honestly, there wasn't
much need for a tour at this point. Besides the kitchen and
combination living room–dining room, there were only
two bedrooms and she'd probably already seen those on
her way down the hall.

Plus, she still hadn't said much directly to him and he
didn't really know what to say either.

He tried to remember what he'd been like at that age.
Sullen and defiant and lonely because his dad was often
out of town working for days at a time, leaving Ethan

alone to fend for himself. Swallowing down his own feelings of resentment, he decided to try a different tactic.

"So, you have a caseworker back home?" he asked.
She'd casually mentioned as much back in the kitchen at
the Cowgirl Up as though it were no big deal. As though
every eleven-year-old had one of those. If she was anything like him, she would try to put on a tough front to
cover how scared she was.

Trina shrugged, but at least it was a response.

So much for the small talk. Ethan took a deep breath,
steeling himself for the tougher questions he knew he
needed to ask. But before he could, she turned to face
him, her eyes narrowed with doubt.

"Were you really a Navy SEAL?"

Okay, so if she wasn't going to talk about herself,
maybe he could lure her into a conversation by letting
down his own guard. "How did you know that?"

"I'm not blind." She pointed to a class picture in a
frame on his fireplace mantel. Besides the small, fake
plant he'd inherited from his dad, it was the only personal item in the room. "It says 'Basic Underwater De-
molition/SEALS Training.' Plus, Chantal already told me
you were in the Navy."

A jolt of surprise caught him, and not just because the
girl referred to her mother by first name. "What else did
your mom tell you about me?"

"That you got her pregnant and then took off."

"Trina…" Ethan took a cautious step forward, dipping
his chin so he could catch her eyes. "I want you to understand that I *never* would've left if I'd known about you." If
she didn't believe anything else about him, he needed her
to know that he'd never intentionally abandoned anyone.

Instead of giving any indication that she heard his

words, Trina pivoted as she studied everything else in the living room but him. "She once told me that you dated anyone in a skirt."

Ethan's throat tightened. Was this how eleven-year-olds talked nowadays? He didn't want to call her mother's honesty into question, but he also didn't like the idea that the deck of lies was already stacked against him. "That's not exactly a fair assessment, considering we only knew each other for a couple of months and we both were in a rush to act like grownups. I was barely eighteen at the time."

"That's how old I'll be in seven years," Trina said without looking at him.

Whoa. He did a double take as he realized she was right. He'd already missed more than half of her childhood, more than eleven birthday parties according to the birth certificate in her bag. "So, you just had a birthday, huh?"

"I guess. You know, this apartment is a total dump."

He followed her gaze down the hall to the second bedroom, which held a creaky twin bed, a cheap dresser and all the cardboard boxes he'd had shipped from his storage unit in San Diego and never got around to unpacking. "Well, it came furnished and I only moved here six months ago. Speaking of which, how did your mom know where to find me?"

That got her attention and her lips went from a pout to a half smirk. "She didn't. I did."

Her admission floored him, but before he could ask how, a knock sounded at the door. If Ethan hadn't already been studying Trina, he would've missed the apprehension flashing through her eyes before she hung her head and focused on the toe of her canvas sneaker again.

When he peeked through the peephole, he recognized Kylie Gregson, Kane's sister, and Mia McCormick. Not only was Kylie related to his boss, she was also the sister-in-law of Ethan's best friend Luke. Kylie and her best friend Mia wouldn't come to his house unless it was for a good reason. A knot formed in his stomach and he glanced back to where Trina was standing. He wanted to communicate to her that he couldn't *not* answer, but his daughter wouldn't lift her face.

Daughter. He was still getting used to that word.

The knock sounded again, this time right against his temple which was resting against the door.

Smothering a groan, Ethan twisted the knob and let the women in.

"We can't stay," Kylie explained, passing him two paper shopping bags with handles. "But we wanted to drop off some stuff for Sugar Falls' newest resident."

If it had been anyone else, Ethan might've thought they were looking for an inside scoop. But he played poker on Thursday nights with both of their husbands and knew the women were sincere.

"What is it?" he asked.

"Mostly a hodgepodge of things a girl might need," Kylie said. Trina must've shown some interest from behind him because one of their unexpected visitors looked past Ethan and spoke to his daughter. "Hi. I'm Kylie Gregson. This is Mia McCormick. She owns the dance studio in town."

Mia lifted up a pink duffel bag. "I know these probably aren't your style, but there aren't a ton of shopping options in Sugar Falls besides the sporting goods store and Designs by Doris, which tends to only carry stuff for the…uh…senior generation, shall we say? Anyway, it was the best we could do on short notice."

The women held up their offerings, but Trina didn't make a move to take anything. She just stood there in her oversize T-shirt and jeans, her blue eyes were fixated on the bags as if they contained explosives. Ethan should've probably accepted them on her behalf, but his brain was still trying to catch up and process how the women not only knew that his daughter needed new stuff, but had gotten everything together so quickly.

"Anyway, I'll be going into Boise this weekend," Kylie said, setting the bags inside the entryway, before she took a retreating step onto the landing outside his front door. "So let me know if you want to pick out some different stuff. I'd be happy to take you shopping, if your dad is okay with that."

With a wink at Ethan, she and Mia were out the door and making their way down the stairs before Ethan could even offer so much as a thanks. He'd yet to think about where he would get suitable clothes for a girl. But apparently, word had already spread about his daughter's unexpected arrival and her meager possessions. For the second time today, he was the last to figure things out and the feeling left him hollow and powerless.

"I guess my mom was right about women wanting to throw themselves at you," Trina finally said before slowly approaching the bags Kylie and Mia had left behind.

The back of his neck prickled in defense. "Those ladies are married to some of my good friends."

Trina shrugged a shoulder, then used a toe to nudge the duffel as though she was looking for a hidden booby trap before she picked it up. Ethan scooped up the bags and carried them the few feet to the ugly orange sofa.

"What about that lady Monica?" Trina asked as she looked longingly at the bags. "Was she just being nice to me because she's married to one of your friends, too?"

"Monica Alvarez isn't married," Ethan replied a bit too

quickly, then cleared his throat. And she most definitely wasn't throwing herself at him. In fact, she'd acted like she couldn't get away from Ethan fast enough this morning. Which was interesting since, normally, she shut him down with a polite shyness or an indifference that made him want to pursue her even more. Today, though, there was an edge to her that he'd never seen and her anger had been solely directed at him. People didn't get mad if they didn't care.

Did that mean that she possibly *did* care about him? A jolt of energy made its way through his bloodstream and a smile tugged at the corners of his lips as he thought of how close she'd stood when she was lecturing him in the corner of the Cowgirl Up kitchen. Of how her breasts had jutted forward when she'd—

"All this stuff is brand-new," Trina said, interrupting the inappropriate turn his thoughts had taken. "It still has tags."

She pulled out a green down jacket in a ladies' size extra-small and a pair of black pants made of a waterproof fabric that looked a few inches too long. There were also a couple of plain, long-sleeved T-shirts and a package of thick socks. Trina held the pink duffel upside down and leggings, a wraparound sweater and some sort of white, strappy tank-top thing that looked like a sports bra fell out. He couldn't be sure because Trina shoved it back into the bag too quickly for Ethan to see, which was just as well.

There was a separate sack at the bottom of one of the brown bags with the name of Lester's Pharmacy on the front. Inside, Trina found a purple toothbrush and an assortment of body lotions and hair products that smelled way more fruity than anything Ethan kept stocked in his bathroom. Every item strewn across his ugly sofa was another reminder that he had absolutely no idea what a girl her age would need.

He racked his brain trying to think of what he'd required when he was that age. Clothes, food—lots of food—a skateboard, music, video games, friends.

"I guess we should probably get you registered for school," he said, and this time he was positive that it was panic that flashed across her face. "What grade are you in?"

"I'm really tired." She shoved the new clothes—the ones he would have to eventually reimburse someone for—onto one cushion at the end of the sofa and plopped down beside them. "Can I take a nap?"

His eyes narrowed at her evasive maneuver to throw him off topic. Although, back when he was that age, he tried to avoid any discussions involving school, as well.

"Yeah. Um, I don't really have the extra room set up just yet, but you can sleep on my bed if you want. Or right here, I guess. Make yourself at home." He knew the platitude sounded forced, but he truly hoped that he could make Trina feel welcome. He just didn't quite know how to do it. "Maybe when you wake up, we can go to the grocery store or something?"

"Whatever," she replied with a yawn before curling into a ball and using the green puffy jacket as a pillow.

It was only ten in the morning and there were still a million questions Ethan wanted to ask her. But she looked depleted and a little lost and, frankly, he didn't even know where to begin. As she dozed on the sofa, Ethan opened one of his kitchen cupboards and took stock of the bare shelves. He debated whether or not he should go to Duncan's Market while his daughter was asleep, but she'd already pulled one vanishing act today. He didn't want to provide her with an opportunity to pull another.

Daughter. There was that word again, although it was coming to his mind with much more frequency considering the fact he still wasn't one hundred percent convinced Trina was his. He used the internet search engine on his smartphone and typed in the letters "DNA," but a wave of guilt crashed into him before he could add the word "test." It felt wrong to even think about blood tests and genetic proof while she was right there in the room, peacefully sleeping after what she'd been through this morning. It wasn't like he would get any answers today, anyway. Even if he did, would it change the fact that her mother had already abandoned her and she had nowhere else to go?

He shoved the phone into the back pocket of his jeans and went into the second bedroom to stare at the dozen or so cardboard boxes piled everywhere. The framed picture on his mantel had been a gift from Luke and Carmen when Ethan had moved to town. The sad-looking silk plant beside it was small enough to fit in his rucksack and served as a reminder that no matter where he went, his old man was always with him.

These boxes held the remaining contents of his life, but he couldn't exactly remember what he'd placed in them before leaving it all in storage. He rolled up his sleeves then hefted one onto his shoulder. He didn't bother opening any of them as he set to work transferring each box to his own bedroom. Whatever was in them obviously wasn't something he'd needed in the past six months. Or even longer, considering he'd likely packed them right after that last deployment that had ended in disaster and resulted in his best friend flying home in a flag-draped casket.

He honestly wasn't sure *what* he needed anymore. All he knew was what he *didn't* need—and that was to have someone else depending on him.

Because the last time he'd been responsible for another person, they'd ended up dying under his watch.

Chapter Four

"Why isn't she in school?" Monica whispered when Ethan walked over to the circulation desk at the library on Thursday afternoon. Freckles sent her a text saying he hadn't come into the Cowgirl Up this morning—as if Monica cared or had all kinds of spare time to add Ethan and his daughter to her already growing list of worries.

Apparently, though, her boss felt the need to keep her apprised of things that weren't her business. And now she was mad at herself for thinking about that text all day. And even madder at the fact that she was currently taking her annoyance out on him.

"I'll get around to registering her eventually," he said, yanking off his thick jacket and revealing his normal uniform of a soft flannel shirt and jeans that fit his slim hips perfectly. "But I'm trying not to rush anything. We're still getting to know each other."

Trina was at least dressed more appropriately for the snowy weather today, so that was a point in Ethan's fatherhood column. Monica jutted her chin toward the bright green coat as it appeared between the YA aisle and the audiobooks. "I see you took her shopping for some new clothes."

"Actually, Kylie and Mia brought that stuff over."

"Then what have you guys been doing the past day and a half?" Monica hated the nosiness of her tone, but she couldn't quash her curiosity.

"Working," Ethan replied simply. She knew he and Kane Chatterson restored Victorian homes and took on general contracting jobs. In fact, she'd hired them to repair one of the walls in Gran's kitchen that had been damaged in a fire last November. The job had only taken a few days and Monica had been able to leave each morning before they'd arrived, returning home long after they were gone.

Which meant she didn't have to gaze at Ethan's muscular body, on full display as he moved around her kitchen like a member of Magic Mike's dance troupe.

"You mean you're taking her to construction sites with you?"

"I don't know what else to do with her."

That brought Monica back to her first question and she wanted to grab hold of the lapels on the man's flannel shirt and give him a good shake. "So then why isn't she in school?"

"I hate school," Trina said, setting down a stack of five books on the checkout desk. She turned to her father and asked, "Do you have a library card?"

Ethan's response was to scrunch his nose, as though his daughter had just asked him if he had four arms. "No. Why would I?"

Her groan was dramatic and typical of most kids her age. "To check out books?"

That's right. When Monica had handed Ethan the copy of *Rejection for Dummies* last week, her tummy had been too tied in knots by his knowing wink and his straight white teeth under his crooked grin. She'd been in such a hurry to get him out of the library, she hadn't even bothered to properly check out the book.

"How do we get Trina a library card?" Ethan asked.

"Fill this out." Monica handed him an application form and one of the stubby golf pencils from the plastic holder by her computer while her eyes stayed on Trina. "Why don't you like school?"

"It's boring. Do you have any of the new books by Veronica Roth?"

"Do you like that series?"

She shrugged. "It's okay."

Monica studied the girl before pointing toward the shelf with the new releases. When Trina was out of earshot, she leaned across the counter at Ethan, who was still completing the application. "Pssst. Did you even look at the books she wants?"

"No. Why?" His face was inches from her, and she could smell the mint on his breath as he whispered back. "Are they inappropriate?"

"What? No. It's just that they're at a high school reading level, which means she must be fairly smart."

"Guess the apple doesn't fall too far from the tree." He winked at her and Monica felt the heat fill her cheeks. It hadn't taken him too long to fall back into his flirtatious comfort zone.

"My point," Monica continued, her jaw tight, "is that she shouldn't be hanging out on construction sites all day."

"Are you saying that smart people can't be found at construction sites?" Something crossed his face and instead of immediately regretting her comment, Monica's blood pumped faster with frustration. She had a feeling he'd purposely chosen to twist her words into an insult.

"Not when they're supposed to be in school, Ethan."

"Maybe I should argue with you more often." His eyes turned a deeper shade, and his knowing smile returned. "I like it when you use my first name."

"Well, I like it when you don't aggravate me beyond all common sense."

"Good to know that I can make you like *something*." Ethan gave a tiny chuckle at her gasp, and then his face grew more serious. "Listen, I'll admit that I don't know the first thing about parenthood. But Trina's been through a lot and I'm doing the best I can. I don't want to push her too much."

Some of the heat died down in Monica's veins as she studied Ethan's face for a sign of sincerity. She wanted to think he had his daughter's best interest at heart, but really, Monica didn't know the guy at all.

"What grade are you in, Trina?" she asked when the girl returned.

"Fifth, I guess."

"You guess?" Monica and Ethan repeated in unison.

Trina shrugged. "I haven't been in a while."

Ethan stood up straighter, the pint-size pencil seeming miniscule in his strong, work-roughened hands. "How long is a while?"

"It's not like I need to go, you guys. I already know most of the stuff the teacher taught, anyway."

"Actually, you *do* need to go," Ethan argued. "It's the law."

"God, now you sound like my truancy officer."

Truancy officer? That must mean the girl had a well-documented history of not attending class. She could see the muscles working in Ethan's jaw as he held himself perfectly still. Hopefully, he wasn't angry with Trina. After all, it wasn't her fault that her mother had been a…a what? Monica swallowed down the judgment.

How did she know what Trina's mother had been through? A kid herself when she'd given birth, and then never seeing the father of her child or getting any help from him whatsoever? What kind of mother would Monica have been in that situation?

"The schools here in Sugar Falls are different," Monica offered because Ethan's frozen-eyed stare suggested he could use a second voice of reason. "I know most of the teachers, and they would probably be willing to work with you if you test into a higher level than the rest of the class."

"You mean like skip a grade?" the girl asked, her eyes flickered with interest.

"I don't know about that, but they have all kinds of programs and opportunities for exceptional students."

Trina's fingers were twitching and Monica saw the girl's feet make small, retreating steps as if she didn't know whether she should take off again. "I don't even have a backpack."

"I'll tell you what," Ethan said. "Why don't we go to the school tomorrow? Monica can call her teacher friends and let them know you're coming. You can take a look around, we can maybe get you registered for those exceptional student classes, and then we'll go down to Boise this weekend and buy some school supplies?"

Exceptional student classes. Monica couldn't believe she'd used that description and she couldn't tell if Ethan knew she'd been improvising that last part. But the fact remained that the child needed to go to school.

"But how will *you* know what I need?" Trina asked Ethan, her voice laced with doubt. Then the girl turned a pair of pleading eyes to Monica. "Would you come shopping with us?"

Monica's voice stuck in her throat and she couldn't form a proper response. After all, she'd been the one to push for the girl to go to school in the first place.

Which was why, two days later, Monica found herself driving down the mountain to Boise with a former Navy SEAL and his new daughter.

Ethan wasn't sure how Trina had done it, but in less than seventy-two hours, she'd accomplished the one thing Ethan hadn't been able to do the past six months—gotten Monica Alvarez to go somewhere in public with him.

Not that it was a date. There was an eleven-year-old riding in the crew cab of his old work truck and, even though his daughter was wearing her headphones and listening to the music she'd figured out how to stream on his smartphone, Trina's presence was chaperone enough.

He'd tried to make conversation with Monica but all she'd seemed to want to discuss was how Trina was feeling—pretty healthy judging by how many groceries she'd already gone through after their initial trip to Duncan's Market; how Trina was adjusting—hard to tell since she rarely said more than a sentence or two at a time; and how the school registration went—much longer than anticipated since Trina skipped out to the girls' bathroom twice during the math assessment test. "I'm starting to wonder if she has a nervous stomach or something."

"Maybe you should take her to see a doctor?" Monica suggested in her quiet librarian voice.

"We have an appointment next week. Mrs. Dunn, the

school nurse, was able to find some vaccination records in the files her old school sent over." Ethan looked in his rearview mirror to ensure Trina was still wearing the headphones before whispering, "From what we gathered, her mother never took her so unless her grandmother got her to a doctor before she passed away, who knows when she last saw any sort of medical professional."

Monica winced. "Any word from the caseworker?"

"Not yet, which has me even more on edge because who knows what I'm going to find out from that report?" The guilt had kept Ethan up every night this week, eating away at him until all he wanted to do was drown out his crippling thoughts with a stiff drink. Flipping on his turn signal with so much force it bounced back into place, Ethan took a deep breath as he eased his foot off the accelerator. "Every time I want to get mad at Chantal for being so damn negligent with my child, I'm faced with the fact that I have no room to talk. At least she was around part of the time and did more than me."

If he'd been hoping that Monica would've said something to ease his guilt, he would have to wait longer. Trina took her earbuds out as he pulled the truck into the parking lot of the Boise Towne Square.

When was the last time he'd gone to an actual mall like this? Even before his shopping destination of choice had changed from the tactical supply store to the local hardware store, Ethan had ordered most of his stuff online. When he did come into the city for essentials, it was for new running shoes or to stock up on work jeans. Obviously, he'd never had to spend much time in the kids' department or the school supply aisle.

Looking at Monica, who was wearing a plain, gray wool coat with her jeans and an old pair of cowboy boots, he got the impression that keeping up with the latest trends wasn't her top priority either. Not that she didn't look great in her clothes, he corrected himself as the muscles in his thighs tightened. Hell, the woman would probably look good in a baggy pair of camo pants. But she was one of those no-nonsense, no-makeup-wearing types. The kind of person who dressed for function, not for fashion.

Maybe that's why his attraction to her grew every time he laid eyes on her. There was definitely something sexy about a woman who didn't have to try too hard, didn't have to flaunt it.

Monica and Trina walked across the parking lot side by side murmuring to each other and Ethan kept behind them. All he could think about was the shape of Monica's denim-clad legs while he counted down the seconds until they got inside and she removed her jacket, giving him a glimpse of her rounded backside in those jeans.

She and Trina might have been talking about which stores they needed to go to first or what they should buy, however, Ethan wanted no part of that strategy. He was just there to hand over his credit card and to carry the bags. When they entered the mall, the blast from the heater—along with Ethan's overactive imagination when it came to Monica's rear end—made him wish he would've left his own coat out in the truck.

"Some of the women in town suggested we go to that juniors store on the first floor," Monica suggested, and the entire way through the shopping center Ethan looked for a safe spot where he could hunker down and wait. Instead, he was forced to follow them into a place where the loud pop music assaulted his eardrums and the cloying, fruity perfume samples assaulted his manhood. He prayed that Monica knew what she was doing.

"I have absolutely no idea what I'm doing," Monica said twenty minutes later when she plopped down beside him on the pink velvet upholstered bench right inside the store. "This has to be the eighth time we've heard this Justin Bieber song and I haven't seen Trina since she went into the dressing room with a stack of clothes."

Ethan sprung up. "Did she take off again?"

"No, I can see her shoes under the door."

"But are they on her feet?"

"Yep. I checked." Monica tapped the side of her head, indicating she was smart enough to already think of that.

"So then why hasn't she picked anything yet?" he groaned, slouching against the glitter painted wood of the bench's backrest.

"I don't know. Some girls get really self-conscious about their bodies around this age. I know I was."

He looked her up and down, desire shooting through him. "Are you kidding? What in the world would you have to be self-conscious about?"

"I didn't always look like this, though. Just like you probably didn't always look like…" A blush stole up Monica's cheeks and he hoped it wasn't just the heat inside the mall.

"Like what?" The corner of his mouth lifted.

"Like a wall of muscle with a little head on top."

"My head's not little." Ethan rubbed at his hair that was longer than regulation. "But feel free to call me a wall of muscle anytime."

"Back to your daughter." Monica rolled her eyes. "I asked her if she needed any help or different sizes, but she insisted she was fine. At first I thought she was nervous about trying the stuff on. But now that I'm thinking about it, she *was* pretty focused on the price tags when we were looking through the racks. She could be worried about how much things cost and what you can afford."

"I can afford it," Ethan replied, his boots firmly planted apart. In fact, being a single guy without many expenses up until now meant that he could afford quite a few shopping sprees.

"That's none of my business. However, maybe you could give Trina a budget so she knows how much she can spend."

"Fine," he muttered as he clenched his fingers into fists and strode deeper into the store as though he was in full tactical gear and had just been briefed on conducting a hostage extraction. Taking note of any alternate exit routes on his way to the fitting rooms, he stealthily steered away from an entire shelf devoted to sequined pillows, averted his eyes when he passed a round clothes rack loaded down with of what could've been white training bras, and then successfully avoided knocking over a display of glitzy BFF necklaces.

"Hey, Trina," he called into the hallway leading toward the partitioned rooms. However, he had to repeat himself to be heard over the pop music blasting from the speakers, the two preteen girls squealing over their matching outfits, and a frazzled-looking mom arguing with her daughter about being too young for something called "booty shorts."

"I don't think she can hear you," Monica said from behind him.

"Well, there's no way any sane guy would willingly step foot past here." Ethan jerked his thumb toward the three-way mirror outside the entrance of the changing area.

"Hey, buddy," a guy with a shaved head whispered conspiratorially and Ethan wanted to sink in relief at the sound of another male voice in this place. "Take it from me, the fuzzy pink bench right by the doors is the closest thing they have to a demilitarized zone. Once they get you to the cash registers, it's too late."

"Can we go to the pretzel place now, Daddy?" A smiling girl about Trina's age looped her arm through the bald man's, forcing the guy to shift the two bags covered in the store's rainbow logo to his free hand.

"Only if they serve tequila there," the guy said, rolling his eyes before smirking at Ethan. "Trust me, you're gonna need a few drinks after you're done here."

"Go on," Ethan called out to the man, staring at the father and daughter as they left. "Save yourself."

Monica swatted at his bicep. But it wasn't just a longing to escape or a desire for a cold cocktail that had caused the weight of envy to settle low in Ethan's belly.

"Do you think Trina will ever look at me like that?" he asked.

"Like what?"

"Never mind." He shook his head and raised his voice as he tried calling for his daughter again. But this time, it came out way too loud and several customers turned to stare while a little boy in a stroller nearby started to cry. Probably because Ethan had just sounded like a recruit division commander shouting at a new recruit.

"Why don't I just go back and get her?" Monica finally offered and Ethan wished he would've just asked her in the first place.

But she didn't have to go very far.

Trina's eyes were wide when she hesitantly came out of the dressing room area and Ethan silently cursed himself for raising his voice earlier and probably startling her. He'd never been afraid of his own old man, probably because Louis Renault was never really home long enough to do much yelling. So it hadn't occurred to him that his own daughter might have anything to legitimately fear from him.

"Honey," Monica said to Trina, before shooting a warning glance at Ethan. Really, neither one of them knew what had happened to her in the past, but surely Monica didn't think he was capable of harming the girl. Did she? "We were just curious to see if you'd found any clothes you like yet."

Trina slowly walked toward them, wearing the same outfit she'd had on when they arrived. Her eyes were downcast and her voice soft when she replied, "I don't know."

He pressed his fingers to his temples, attempting to stimulate his brain for something to say that would take the sting out of his earlier tone. "You know, Trina, all the other girls in the store are finding clothes they like."

This brought his daughter's head up. "Do you wish I was more like the other girls?"

"No. I want you to be yourself. That's why I brought you here. So that you could pick out your *own* clothes."

Trina's face dropped. "But I don't know what I'm allowed to pick."

"Well, Ethan… I mean…your dad said that he didn't care about the prices." Monica got behind Ethan and used her shoulder to nudge the back of his bicep, making him step forward.

Technically, he *had* said that, but it wasn't like he wanted to throw his money away either. He tried not to pat the pocket containing his wallet. "If it's something you like and if you'll wear it, then let's get it."

His daughter's smile was shy and tentative at first, but when Monica nodded encouragement at the girl, Ethan realized he couldn't place a monetary value on his daughter's happiness.

Or on the feeling of Monica pressed up against his side.

* * *

A few hundred dollars later, Ethan realized that he might've gone a little overboard during a shopping spree that didn't involve a single infrared light, combat boot or armor plate. Monica had tried to warn him that he should pace himself because there were only so many hoodies an eleven-year-old needed.

"You might want to ask the cashier about signing up for their rewards program for future discounts," Monica suggested under her breath when Ethan handed over his credit card. "You'll have to do this all over again when the summer clothes come out."

Ethan gulped at the thought of making a return trip to the mall again in a couple of months. Not that he'd minded buying things for his daughter. Hell, he hadn't ever bought so much as a diaper, let alone paid child support. So a new wardrobe barely even put a dent in his guilty conscience or made up for all lost time. He just didn't want to have to be present for the process of trying on everything all over again and deciding whether to go with the denim popover dress or the flutter sleeve romper.

God, he hated the fact that he now knew what a romper was.

"No problem," he said, trying to scoop up all six large shopping bags off the counter at once. Trina was quick to grab the one he'd missed and held it close to her torso. It was the same way he'd carried his first set of Navy dress blues back to the barracks. Ethan had earned that uniform and it was the first item of clothing he'd ever had tailored especially for him. He'd grown a few sizes since then, but he still had the thing carefully packed away in one of his boxes at home.

So instead of insisting on carrying all the bags, Ethan

decided to let his child have her own moment of pride for something new. He winked at Trina before asking, "Should we go get some gedunk?"

She scrunched up her nose. "What's that?"

"Some junk food. Like a snack to reward ourselves for getting through this."

Trina nodded and all but skipped out into the mall, as though trying on all those clothes hadn't completely wiped her out. Hell, all he'd done was sit there on that stupid, safe pink bench and nod his approval, yet he was completely exhausted.

Monica hung back with Ethan as they followed the girl's lead toward the food court. He'd hoped that it was because the woman simply enjoyed his company, and he was about to switch his smile back on and say as much. However, when his daughter was out of earshot, it was clear she had something else on her mind. "You should also keep in mind that kids this age start going through their growth spurts and many of these things might not fit her next school year."

Ethan paused midstep. It was the first time he'd realized that this fatherhood deal wasn't just a one and done kind of deal. Obviously, he knew that it was a long-term responsibility, but he'd never really thought of it as more than a series of tasks. Like spec ops missions, you finish one assignment and move on to the next—a new adventure always around the corner. He hadn't quite been anticipating a repeating cycle. Like shopping. Thinking of the bald guy from earlier today made him scratch at his own head. How did other dads get through this over and over again?

Using his thumb to push against the throbbing in his temple, Ethan muttered, "I could really use something stronger than a pretzel."

Chapter Five

"What about shoes?" Trina asked around a mouthful of cinnamon-and-sugar-covered soft pretzel. Monica hadn't thought it was possible for Ethan's eyes to get any rounder today and she had to choke back a giggle at his terrified expression.

"Yeah, we should probably check out the sneaker place next." Monica pushed up her sleeves. "I'm ready to do more damage there as soon as your father is."

Yet, when Ethan remained in an apparent state of shock, Monica fluttered her lashes at him and said, "Just blink twice for yes."

"I thought we were done." He held up his plastic cup of frozen lemonade. "See, this was my reward for not going totally insane in the last store."

"That's okay," Trina murmured, tucking in her chin. "These shoes will work."

Monica followed the child's gaze to the small hole in the canvas over the big toe. She opened her mouth to chastise Ethan for his complete disregard in handling his daughter's disappointment.

But the man must've recognized the defeated expression on the girl's face because he quickly spoke up. "No, you need something more sturdy. More suited for the weather here in the mountains. And we should also get you a pair of shoes to go with that romper dress thing you picked out."

Trina's eyes lifted, flickering with hope, and Monica didn't have the heart to correct Ethan and tell him that it was really Monica who'd picked out the dress. The girl was happy with jeans and solid-colored T-shirts and sweaters. Yet, Gran always insisted that every female needed a fancier outfit for those special occasions. Not that Monica remembered the last time she'd dressed up in Sugar Falls.

The first hour of shopping had her questioning her own sanity for agreeing to run interference between Ethan and his long-lost daughter. By the time they shoved the last shoe box and bags of school supplies into the crew cab of the truck later that afternoon, though, her nerves were a little less frayed as she basked in the afterglow of a job well done.

It would've felt like a regular family outing if the three of them had any trust or confidence in the others. Unfortunately, Monica still didn't trust Ethan not to shirk his responsibilities, and Ethan didn't trust Trina not to run off, and Trina didn't quite trust anyone. Yet. But she was coming around.

As Ethan pulled onto the two-lane highway, Trina had retreated into her headphones with her music and Monica watched the sun dip lower behind the snow-covered mountains.

"So that went better than I expected," he said quietly, mirroring her own thoughts.

"Yeah, it was touch and go there for a while." Monica smiled at him, but when he returned it with a wicked grin of his own, the corner of her lip trembled. Really, the man's mouth should come with its own warning. *Caution: smirking leads to increased knee weakening.*

"I really started sweating when we walked by that booth that did the ear piercing. Thankfully, you came through and steered her toward the bookstore."

"Girls like me and Trina would rather have a new book than a pair of earrings any day."

"Yeah, you guys remind me of each other in a lot of ways."

Oh geez, did he just compare her to his eleven-year-old daughter? Or was that Monica who'd drawn the comparison? In the past few months, she'd grown accustomed to Ethan always flirting with her. Yet, ever since Trina arrived, it was like something had completely changed in his whole demeanor. Sure, he still stared at Monica when he thought she wasn't looking, but it was no longer in that playful, out-to-have-a-good-time way he used to look at her. He might throw out a bold wink here and there, but it now seemed like those were only for show, to pretend as if his whole life hadn't suddenly changed and grown more complicated.

While it made sense that he was completely out of his element with this unexpected role of fatherhood, and she should want him to be taking his responsibilities seriously, there was a teeny tiny hole right below Monica's chest that missed his more happy-go-lucky personality.

And she could hardly believe it.

"Like how?" Monica finally asked.

"Huh?" he replied, apparently lost in his own thoughts. Before Trina arrived, she never would've pinned Ethan as the quiet and contemplative type.

"How do we remind you of each other?" she clarified.

"Well, you guys are both kind of quiet and shy, but incredibly smart. Like I know there's got to be so much going on in your brain, but for the life of me, I can't figure out what you're thinking. Still, I find myself wanting to know everything about you." He lifted up his sunglasses as he cast a glance across the cab of the truck and Monica squirmed in the passenger seat. "I want to know what makes you happy, what makes you sad, what makes you tick."

"It's going to take time for you to get to know Trina like that," Monica said as she tugged on the shoulder strap of her seat belt, trying to give her neck a little relief from this sudden tightness. What she hadn't added was that Ethan had no hope of ever getting to know Monica like that. Sure, there might be times when she would lower her defenses, but she would never let her guard down with him. Or with any man ever again.

"She warmed up for a while there at the mall." Ethan glanced at his rearview mirror and then lowered his voice, forcing Monica to lean toward the center console to hear him better. "But then when we went to the office supply store, she got super withdrawn and wouldn't even make eye contact."

"I'm surprised you noticed that."

"Give me a little credit, Mon," Ethan said, his use of the shortened version of her name causing a tingling sensation in her rib cage. Great. Going on a family shopping trip with him had already created a false sense of intimacy between them. "Just because I'm uncomfortable dealing with female moods doesn't mean that I don't pay attention to them. Especially when it concerns someone I care about."

Monica tried not to look toward the backseat. It would've been a sure sign to Trina that they were talking about her. "My guess is that shopping for clothes and shoes is fun, but buying paper and pencils is a reminder that she's going to have to go to school soon. I wonder why that makes her so apprehensive."

"Probably because it's school." Ethan shrugged. "No kids I knew ever enjoyed going."

"I think it might be something more than that. Maybe she struggled with bullies at her old school or has a learning disability that makes the work tough for her."

"But you said her reading level was well above average."

"She could still struggle in other areas academically or even socially. Or maybe she had behavioral issues and used to get in trouble a lot?"

"If that's the case, the apple *really* wouldn't be falling far from the tree." His grin was finally back and Monica's heart sped up as he turned into the driveway of her grandmother's old house.

"Oh look," Trina said, pointing to the older woman standing near the snow-covered woodpile wearing a pair of patent leather tap shoes and a faded bathrobe that only came to her knobby knees. "I didn't know you guys had a kitten."

"Neither did I," Monica grumbled as she hopped out of the passenger side before Ethan could put the truck in Park.

* * *

Despite the fact that Monica had already been outside at the end of her driveway when they'd picked her up this morning, Ethan had still planned on walking her to her front door this evening. But when he saw Mrs. Alvarez standing outside in the snow with a kitten in her arms, he realized they might be here for longer than he'd anticipated.

He and Kane had done most of the repair work on the house when Mrs. Alvarez caught a frozen pizza on fire a few months ago and, after spending several days with the older woman, he knew two things. One, she didn't have a cat. Two, she only wore those fifty-year-old dance shoes when she was having one of her "episodes."

But it was Trina who got to the older woman first. "Can I hold your kitten?"

"Sure," Mrs. Alvarez replied as she handed over a ball of gray fur to his daughter. "But she's still a little sore from getting her shots today so be careful."

"Gran, did you find that cat in the woodpile?"

"What woodpile?" she asked her granddaughter. Monica pointed to the split logs stacked against the entire side of the smaller Victorian home. "Oh, that's right. The ol' furnace kept growling and hissing so much, it gave poor kitty a bad case of gas. So we came out here to get some wood for a fire."

Monica took off her glasses before pinching the bridge of her nose. Ethan cleared his throat, wanting to help ease some of her frustration. "Hey, Mrs. Alvarez, remember you promised Chief Jones that you wouldn't use the fireplace or the oven unless Monica was home."

"But she *is* home." Mrs. Alvarez gave him a dismissive wave as though her granddaughter had been there all along and hadn't just arrived with Ethan. "Wait until you try her enchiladas, Mr. Renault. It's a family recipe and she makes them just like my own *mami* did. *Mija*, is dinner ready yet?"

"Not yet, Gran," Monica said, her exhale louder than the wind whistling through the pine needles on the ancient evergreen tree near the driveway. She wrapped an arm around her grandmother's hunched shoulders. "Come on, let's go inside and get warmed up."

Trina was cooing at the kitten and, for the millionth time today, all Ethan could do was stand there frozen, unsure of what to do. If this was a hostage extraction or the detonation of an IED, he'd be much more comfortable. Being a rescuer came as easily to him as breathing. Unfortunately, he wasn't sure who needed to be rescued first—Monica or her poor, confused Gran. In his mind, he heard his BUD/S instructor's voice telling him, *Adapt and overcome.*

When his gaze fell on the wood he asked his daughter, who seemed oblivious to anything but the purring fuzz ball curled up in her hands, "Do you mind if we stay for a few minutes so I can get a fire started for them?"

"Sure. Can we have some enchiladas, too?"

Ethan grabbed a couple of logs. "I don't think there's actually any enchiladas. Mrs. Alvarez gets confused easily and must've forgotten that Monica was with us all day."

"Too bad. I'm getting kind of bored going out to eat all the time." Trina sniffed before she followed behind the two women who'd just gone into the house.

Okay, so maybe she wasn't the only one who was tired of takeout. Ethan made a mental note to learn how to make a home-cooked meal. If he could construct an improvised explosive device in the middle of an overgrown jungle or a barren desert, surely he could manage something basic. There had to be cookbooks at the library. And if not, he could always find a YouTube video to show him how.

As he knelt in front of the fireplace, he heard the two women talking in the kitchen. Their voices weren't raised, so at least nobody was yelling or seemed to be otherwise flustered. Once he finished lighting the fire, he stood up to tell them that he and Trina were going to take off.

Passing the fridge, he saw the whiteboard affixed to the front of it. Someone had used a red dry erase marker to write, "Monica is in Boise today and will be home at 6:00 p.m. Mr. Simon is next door if you need him."

"Excuse me," Monica said, brushing past him and opening the freezer to pull out a foil-covered dish. Ethan gulped, partly from her nearness and partly from his hope that she might actually be making enchiladas. Would it be horribly rude of him to swing an invite for dinner when she so clearly had her hands full dealing with her grandmother's dementia?

"So, Gran, where did you find the cat?" Monica asked as she put the frozen dish into the oven.

"I picked her up at the animal shelter this morning." Gran was sitting at the kitchen table, a blanket across her lap and the toes of her dance shoes tapping against the hardwood floor Ethan had just resanded a few months ago.

"The shelter on the way to Boise?" Monica couldn't hide the panic that flashed across her face. "Who took you there?"

From what Ethan understood, Mrs. Alvarez had lived in this house for the past forty years and had been a member of every organization and club in town. She must have friends and neighbors who were willing to take her places and help out when Monica wasn't with her.

"I drove myself." She pulled a single key out of her robe pocket and set it down on the table next to the mug of steaming water in front of her. "I found the spare in your bedroom."

"You took my car?" Monica dropped the box of chamomile tea she'd just pulled down from the cabinet. "Gran, you don't have a license anymore. You're lucky you didn't crash into someone else—oh my gosh, you didn't get in an accident did you?"

"*Mija*, I've been driving since I was thirteen years old and never had an accident."

Monica squeezed her eyes shut and took several deep breaths before she responded.

"You caused that big pileup on the highway two years ago, remember? That's why Dr. Wu took your license away." Her voice was strained, but way more reasonable than Ethan's would have been under the same circumstances.

Instead of nodding in understanding, Mrs. Alvarez rolled her eyes. "I don't even know a Dr. Wu. Your grandfather and I have always seen Dr. Jorgensen."

Ethan immediately went to retrieve the forgotten box at Monica's feet and heard her murmuring to herself. "It's probably pointless to tell her that both my grandfather and Dr. Jorgensen passed away before I was born."

He fished a tea bag out and plopped it into Mrs. Alvarez's mug of hot water. As he returned the box to the cabinet beside Monica, he lowered his own voice. "Why don't I go outside and check your car for any damage?"

"You don't have to. I can handle it." He recognized

when someone was trying to cover up and pretend they were capable of handling something themselves, despite all evidence pointing to the contrary. Hadn't he done the same thing—*said* the same thing—all those times before he'd decided to get sober?

"I know you can handle it and I wasn't implying otherwise. But we can all use an extra hand from time to time."

She tilted her head as she studied him, her left cheek sucked in as his offer hung between them. He could see the struggle behind her proud eyes and knew she was pondering whether or not she should accept his help. Whether she should rely on someone else for a change, especially a guy who had his own battles.

Ethan experienced an intense need to prove to her that he wasn't completely useless. "Mon, I can't even begin to repay you for helping me at the mall today with Trina. This is the least I can do."

Monica sighed. "Fair enough. But then we're even."

Ethan grinned at her before snatching the spare key off the table. He didn't bother pointing out that, with the way Monica and Trina had already bonded over books and shopping, he doubted that today wasn't going to be the last favor he'd have to ask of her.

Monica took Gran upstairs to change, sitting the tiny woman down on the bed so she could remove the tap shoes first. "Make sure you put them back in their special box, *mija*."

As if Monica hadn't had to put the patent leather heels away at least four times a week with these forgetful episodes coming more frequently. She studied the shoes in the worn-out shoe box with the faded Capezio logo on the top. Gran had been quite the dancer back in her day and had several VHS movies downstairs where one could catch a glimpse of Lydia Alvarez in the background as part of the ensemble cast. She even had a signed photograph of her with Elvis Presley from that time she'd been an extra in a beach party scene.

She wished Ethan could see how Gran used to be. *She wasn't always like this*, Monica often found herself explaining to random strangers in town who didn't know that her sweet and intelligent grandmother would never have tap-danced in the middle of Town Square Park wearing just her bathrobe if the woman was still in control of her faculties. Lydia Alvarez had been strong and capable and the life of the party up until a few years ago. But those glimpses of the same woman were decreasing with alarming frequency, and soon Monica herself might forget what the younger Gran was like.

Monica's loud sigh didn't alleviate any of the heaviness in her heart. By the time she returned from the closet, Gran was fast asleep on top of her blankets. Luckily, her grandmother only weighed about a hundred pounds, so while Monica couldn't lift her, she could maneuver her enough to pull the quilt out from underneath and cover her up. Standing at the doorway, she watched her grandmother sleep.

"Oh, Gran, what am I going to do with you?"

The only answer she got was a soft snore. Turning off the light, Monica squared her shoulders before heading back downstairs.

When she walked into the kitchen, she found Ethan pacing in front of the brand-new oven while Trina sat at the old Formica-covered table, holding a sleeping kitten in her arms. Apparently, it was too much to hope that the man would've done what most people do when faced with

Gran's odd behavior—pretend they hadn't noticed anything out of the ordinary and then politely find an excuse to leave as quickly as possible.

"Is everything okay?" he asked as soon as he saw her.

"Yeah. Gran fell asleep."

He shot a look toward Trina, then lowered his voice. "Is it Alzheimer's?"

Monica nodded. "She usually just wanders down the street or talks an unsuspecting passerby into a ride to town, but this is the first time she's ever taken off in my car."

"Speaking of which, there were a few little scratches and dings but it was tough for me to tell if any of it was recent." Ethan's words were a diplomatic way of saying that her Toyota Camry was nearly fifteen years old and had definitely seen better days. However, it was all she could afford when every extra dime she made went into a savings account for Gran's future medical expenses. "You might want to go out to the driveway and check to see if you recognize anything new."

The timer on the stove went off right then, making her already frazzled nerve endings pulse with each shriek of the buzzer. The last thing Monica wanted right that second was company. After all, it was much easier to pretend that nothing was wrong with her closest living relative when she didn't have an audience. But Gran took great pride in feeding any and everyone who crossed her doorstep and would be disappointed if Monica didn't offer their guests something to eat.

"Would you guys like some enchiladas? There's more than en—"

"Yes, please," Trina said rather loudly, not even letting Monica finish. She knew Ethan ate most of his meals out, so the girl's enthusiasm was probably only the result of the chance to have a home-cooked dinner.

"I don't want to impose…" Ethan's words faded as she lifted the foil off the pan and the air filled with the scent of the rich, spicy sauce.

Monica looked over her shoulder to see him staring hungrily at the cheese-covered tortillas. His front teeth scraped against his lower lip and her pulse sped up. What would it feel like to have him look at her like that? What would those teeth feel like if they lightly scraped the sensitive skin right below her…

She shivered wistfully before giving her head a quick shake. Nope. There was no point in even thinking about something so reckless. With his daughter here, Monica had been doubling her efforts to distance herself from the man. Clearly she would need to work harder at it.

Shoving the pot holders at him, she instructed, "Here, put this on the table and I'll get the plates and silverware."

"Trina, why don't you set the kitten down while we eat?" Ethan told his daughter. The girl gently put the sleeping kitty on the red vinyl chair next to her, then stood up to wash her hands at the sink.

Serving her guests gave Monica a task to focus on, even if she did so a little distractedly. She tried to pretend she was at her waitressing job and not in her own kitchen. But she never had to sit at the table with the customers while they ate, so the conversation soon stalled after a few bites.

Well, the kitten's conversation didn't stall. Apparently, as soon as it was separated from the warmth of Trina's arms, the tiny thing woke up—and didn't like being away from her holder one little bit. She meowed louder and louder until Trina lifted it off the seat and tucked the animal into the wide front pocket of her new hooded sweatshirt.

"So, what are you going to do about your grand-mother?" Ethan finally asked, echoing the same question Monica had asked herself upstairs. "I mean, do you have any plans for what happens down the road?"

"I know I'll have to do something eventually..." she started, then glanced at Trina unsure of how much she should say in front of the child. The bottom line was that Gran's condition would only get worse.

"I think they have special homes," Ethan offered. "A few weeks ago we did some work on this old fisherman's cabin to get it ready to sell. His kids were moving him to a place called a memory care center."

"I know. I've looked into it. But it's not what we do in my family. I have a cousin in El Paso and when he put my aunt Bettina in a place, nobody else in the family would invite him to a backyard cookout, let alone a wedding. Besides, Gran took me and my mom in after my dad left us. When my mom passed away, Gran raised me. She gave up her golden years to care for me. The least I can do is return the favor."

"Maybe you can hire a nurse or something to be with her when you're at work?" Ethan's suggestion was probably well-intentioned, but it made the skin on the back of her neck prickle. Did he seriously think she hadn't already researched all the options? Anytime she had a down moment at the library, all she did was research.

"I've also looked into that. Even with Gran's social security and both of my jobs, I could only afford about two hours a day."

A meow sounded from Trina's midsection, drawing Monica's attention back to the current crisis at hand. She took her glasses off and set them on the table so she could relieve some of the tension building in her temples, as well as prevent her from clearly seeing the adorable kitten's face when she said, "I'm going to have to call the animal shelter tomorrow and find out what their return policy is."

Trina gasped, looking at Monica as if she'd suggested tying the kitten into a burlap bag and throwing it out into the middle of Lake Rush. Monica tried not to shrink any lower in her chair.

"Honey, it's not that I don't *want* the kitten. I'd love to have a pet. But Gran is always misplacing things and then can't remember where she left them. When I'm at work all day, I'll often come home to find her snow boots in the fridge, and the sandwich I'd made for her lunch on the floor in the mudroom. As much as she'd love to, my grandmother simply can't take care of a young, helpless kitten." Monica dragged in another deep breath. "I can't believe the people at the shelter actually let her adopt it in the first place."

"Your gran looks healthy to me." Trina tilted her head. "Is something wrong with her?"

"Physically, she's totally fine. The only medication she takes is for her high blood pressure. Other than that, she's in great shape physically. But her brain is starting to shut down and she gets confused easily and is always forgetting things, like turning off the stove before something catches fire or not watching for cars when she walks into town…in the middle of the night. I worry that she could be a danger to herself."

"My gran was the opposite," Trina said, setting down her fork after finishing the entire plate of enchiladas. "Her brain remembered everything and she was always supersmart. But she had bad knees and couldn't walk and then she got real sick and went to the hospital. I never saw her after that."

"That must have been very sad for you," Ethan said to the girl, who was using her finger to give the kitten a tiny nibble of leftover cheese. "I only met your gran two or three times when I picked up your mom for dates, but she would be sitting on her front porch working on a cross-word with a plate of homemade treats beside her. She used to make the best brownies I've ever had."

When it came to his daughter, Ethan usually was at a loss for words and Monica hadn't expected him to be the one to offer comfort. Yet, sharing a happy memory of Trina's grandmother had been the perfect response. Something warm spread through Monica's chest as she studied the pair across the table.

"Chantal said Gran died because she ate too many sweets and never exercised." The fact that Trina referred to her own mother by first name chipped away at Monica's prior sympathy for the woman who'd given birth to Ethan's child. "Chantal was always worried about getting fat like Gran. That's why she took a special medicine to keep herself skinny all the time."

Monica's own father hadn't been a part of her life be-cause he used to prefer taking a special medicine, too. The way Ethan's face had gone pale suggested that Chantal's choice of pharmaceuticals was of the same variety and was most likely illegal. While Fidel Alvarez only showed up sporadically for the occasional childhood events, at least Monica had a few good memories of her dad being loving toward her. Of him bringing her a new book and a candy ring pop before he would lift her up in his strong arms and tease that she was growing too big too quickly.

Until the last time Monica saw him, when he didn't take her in his arms at all.

Ethan cleared his throat and Monica didn't blame him for wanting to change the subject. "I bet that if you call the shelter and explain what happened, they could find a new home for the kitten."

"I can take care of Tootie."

Ethan's head whipped to the side to stare at his daughter. "Who?"

"Tootie." Trina nodded toward the kitten that was now licking red sauce off her finger. "I've been calling her that because she seems to have the toots."

Monica wrinkled her nose. "Maybe we shouldn't feed her any more enchiladas."

"Um…but you'll be at school and I'm at work," Ethan replied, not seemingly bothered by the animal's gas issues. His eyes darted back and forth between Monica and his daughter as if he was hoping someone would intervene and be the voice of reason. "Remember Monica said the kitten shouldn't be alone during the day?"

Instead of throwing him a life rope, Monica seized on the opportunity to not have to call the shelter and look like a big, evil animal hater.

"I didn't say the kitten couldn't be alone. I said I couldn't leave *Gran* alone with her." *Please don't ask me for more details than that*, Monica thought. She would hate to have Trina hear the story about how Gran found two baby skunks last spring and thought the neighbor's untrained German shepherd wouldn't bark so much if it had some new playmates. Fortunately, Mr. Simon had heard the initial growling and ran outside right away. Unfortunately, neither he nor Rambo were safe from the spray when the mama skunk swooped in to save her babies. When Gran later realized what she'd nearly done, she'd been inconsolable for days. "Cats are actually very independent and can pretty much take care of themselves."

Ethan narrowed his eyes at Monica but she quickly stood up and began occupying herself with clearing the table and taking the empty casserole pan to the sink.

"Please, can we keep Tootie?"

Even from all the way across the kitchen, Monica heard the air whoosh out of Ethan's mouth. As far as she could tell, it was the first time the child had actually asked him directly for something, rather than wait for him to offer it. Trina's request meant that she was becoming more comfortable with him.

Perhaps it was wrong to use Ethan's vulnerability with this new role of fatherhood against him, but Monica really didn't want to take the poor kitten back to the shelter. After all, it was *her* fault that she'd left her car key where Gran could find it. That made her equally responsible for finding Tootie a new home.

"Having a pet *does* teach children about responsibility." Monica looked at Ethan over the lenses of her glasses and attempted a big smile that felt completely unnatural. "It can also make them feel more secure in a new place."

"When you two tag team me like that, I don't stand a chance," Ethan groaned. "Fine, Tootie can stay at our house."

He stood up to carry his plate to the sink and Trina's whoops kept her from hearing her father when he lowered his voice, his breath caressing Monica's ear as he whispered, "But man, you're gonna owe me for this one."

Monica shivered, wondering if she'd just made a deal with the devil.

Chapter Six

"So I go to school tomorrow and then what?" Trina asked as she sat on her bed with Tootie on Sunday evening, both of them watching Ethan fix a broken drawer on her dresser so that she could finish organizing and putting away all her new clothes.

Despite being in the military for nearly ten years and accustomed to following so many rules and regulations, Ethan preferred to fly by the seat of his pants. His daughter, on the other hand, was proving to be more schedule oriented. So far today, he'd had to lay out their plans for breakfast (grabbing doughnuts at the bakery), their plans for church (he didn't attend, but apparently her grandmother had been a stickler for going every Sunday morning) and their plans for purchasing cat supplies (the pet store visit an hour ago was only slightly less overwhelming than their excursion to the mall yesterday).

But at least she was opening up and talking with him a little more.

"I'll be standing outside of the school when the bell rings at three o'clock. Maybe we can go get an ice cream at Noodie's afterward."

Seeing all the bright colored tops and leggings out of their bags really made the rest of the spare bedroom look pretty nondescript and bare. Maybe he should've let her pick out a new bedspread or something to spruce things up.

"And then what?"

"Um, you tell me about your day, I guess?" Should he already be enrolling her in sports or piano lessons or whatever it was that kids did after school?

"Okay. What happens after that?"

"Then we grab some dinner and I usually go to a meeting on Monday nights."

"What kind of meeting?" Trina asked. She was holding one of her new shoelaces up, watching Tootie bat a paw at it.

As much as he didn't want to say anything that might make him sound bad, part of his recovery was honesty. "I used to drink too much."

"You mean…" Suddenly, his daughter's animated expression grew hesitant. Perhaps even nervous.

"I'm talking about alcohol. Do you know what I mean?"

Trina bit her lip as she lowered the shoelace and looked down, refusing to meet his gaze as she slowly nodded.

Ethan dropped to his knees in front of her, needing her to see how serious he was. "Listen, I don't drink alcohol anymore. But it's important for me to go to meetings and talk with other people who have the same issue so we can support each other. Help each other stay healthy. Does that make sense?"

Trina lifted her chin just enough so she could study him out of the eye that wasn't covered behind her loose hair. "The judge told Chantal that she needed to go to meetings like that. But she had to live at rehab houses for *her* meetings and told Gran it was too hard to stay in places like that. Do you have to move into rehab, too?"

"No." Ethan flinched at being lumped in the same category as his former prom date, who he'd suspected of being strung out on something the day she'd left Trina on his doorstep. It'd been confirmed when the girl had mentioned Chantal using a "special medicine" to keep from gaining weight. "My meetings are voluntary—that means nobody forces me to go—and they only last an hour. I go once or twice a week."

Sometimes more often if he thought he needed it. Or on days when he was especially antsy or restless or in need of an outlet.

"Do I go to the meeting with you?" Trina toyed with the end of the shoelace, making Tootie think that the batting game was starting back up.

"Um, I've never seen kids there. I can ask, though. If it is something you really want to do, maybe we can get permission for you to come with me once in a while. Or we can just stay home tomorrow night. It's okay if I miss once in a while."

"No. Meetings are important," Trina said. Her voice was usually serious, but this time, it held a note of urgency, as well. "Whenever my… Chantal forgot to go to hers, we wouldn't see her for months."

The poor girl had already lost everything she'd loved. He couldn't very well allow her to worry about him falling off the wagon, too. She deserved having some stability in her life. "If it's important to you, Trina, I won't miss any meetings. We can figure everything out. You don't know this about me yet, but I'm really good at making things work."

"Maybe I can go to the library tomorrow night and hang out with Monica?"

"I think the library closes at six." Ethan stood up to pull his phone out of his pocket to check the hours online.

"Then maybe I could go to her house for dinner? She has good food there and I'll take Tootie so her grandmother can play with her and get some cuddles."

He had to admit it wasn't a bad idea. But could Ethan really impose upon the Alvarez family again?

Last night, when he'd told Monica that she would owe him, he hadn't really meant it. He just wanted to let her know that he knew what she was doing by giving the kitten to Trina, and that he might expect some appreciation from her in return. Actually, he'd prefer some cuddles of his own, but he wasn't in any sort of position to be looking for a date right now. Which was really too bad, because he'd actually enjoyed being with Monica yesterday. Don't get him wrong, he still hated the shopping. But she was so calm through it all, so understanding of what his daughter needed—of what *he* needed—that for the first time in months, Ethan didn't have to pretend he knew what he was doing. Working with Monica was the closest he'd gotten to being a member of a team since he'd left the Navy. And she was definitely the most attractive teammate he'd ever had, with her sweet dimples and her silky brown curls and her curvy...

Ugh. Ethan had been so caught up in thoughts of Monica, his phone screen had gone dark and he had to reenter his pass code, only to realize that he'd forgotten what he'd been looking up in the first place. He really needed to put that attraction on hold while he figured out what was best for Trina.

There were plenty of other people in town that he would trust to babysit Trina, but his daughter didn't know any of them. She was probably too young to stay home alone. As if reading his thoughts, she suggested, "I could just stay here by myself. After my grandma died, I lived in worse neighborhoods with Chantal and she would leave me by myself all the time."

That was it. Ethan gripped his phone tighter, determined to be the exact opposite type of parent as Chantal. They'd exchanged numbers at the mall in case anyone got lost so he already had Monica's contact info handy to type out a text. I have a really huge favor and you can say no. But I have a meeting tomorrow and can't take Trina. Is there any way she can come to your place?

He used the camera feature to snap a quick image of his daughter playing with the kitten, partly for the adorable factor (as in, *How could anyone say no to this?*) and partly to remind the woman that he'd already prepaid the favor by taking in this animal with gastrointestinal issues.

Speaking of Tootie's gas, Ethan should probably grab a can of air freshener at the market and send a picture of that to Monica, as well. Just so she could see the extent of his sacrifice for dealing with this unexpected pet.

It took another ten minutes—and several muffled curse words—for Ethan to get the dresser drawer back on the track. When he did, he was rewarded with a small grin from Trina, who was eager to finish putting away her new clothes.

Walking out of the room with his tool bag, he was also

rewarded with a text from Monica, whose straightforward "Sure" and smile emoji might have been intended as a polite response.

But that simple response also sent a tiny spark of adrenaline through him.

"Is this the sweet Trina I've been hearing all about?" Freckles boomed out when Ethan and his daughter came into the Cowgirl Up Café early Monday morning.

"Yes, ma'am," Ethan replied, and Monica witnessed his chest puff out with a bit more pride than it had the last time he'd walked through the restaurant's saloon-style doors. "Freckles, this is my daughter, Trina. Trina, allow me to introduce you to the owner of this fine establishment and the person who knows everything about what's going on in town."

"Fine establishment" might be a stretch, Monica thought, as she looked around at the bright turquoise walls covered with neon painted lassos, bedazzled horseshoes and enough cowgirl paraphernalia to host a rodeo-themed party inside every sorority house at Boise State. But her part-time boss and the popular café were definitely the center for gossip in Sugar Falls.

In fact, Freckles had been good friends with Gran for years and was the first one to point out to Monica that her grandmother might be suffering from something more than absentmindedness. A couple of years ago, it had been easy for Monica to miss the signs herself because she lived with the older woman and the changes were so gradual, it was easy to grow immune to the forgetfulness and write off the initial episodes as occasional quirkiness.

Freckles was also the one who suggested that Monica might need to start saving for Gran's health care down the road, and offered up a few extra shifts at her restaurant, despite the fact that Monica wasn't very outgoing and pretty much sucked at being a waitress at first.

"Nice to finally meet you, Trina," Freckles said around the wad of chewing gum in her mouth. "Your dad is one of my best customers, so I knew he couldn't keep you away from my famous cinnamon rolls for too long. Have a seat and I'll bring a couple out."

Trina gave a shy nod, but instead of keeping her eyes downcast she turned to look around the room, her gaze landing on Monica. "Oh! Hi."

"Hey, guys," Monica said, walking to their table with a pot of coffee. "Are you all ready for the first day of school?"

"Not really," Trina replied, her shoulders slumping under the new green jacket. "Are you sure I can't just hang out at the library and read? That's pretty much the same thing as going to school."

"Sorry, kiddo," Monica said with a sympathetic smile. "But you can come to the library after school if you want and tell me all about your day."

The girl sighed. "I can tell you about it right now. It's gonna be horrible and I'm gonna hate it."

"I hated being stuck in a classroom when I was your age, too," Freckles said, returning to the table with two fresh cinnamon rolls slathered in cream cheese frosting. "But I sure loved recess. All the boys would chase us around the playground and, sometimes, I'd even let the cute ones catch me."

Monica rolled her eyes and took her order pad out of her apron pocket. "So what can I get you for your big first day of school feast?"

"Well, we've been stocking up on cereal and Pop-Tarts

at the market lately," Ethan said, explaining why they hadn't been in for breakfast since the day Trina arrived. "So preferably something hot. Trina, do you want a few minutes to look over the menu?"

"I don't really feel like eating." The girl scooted out of the booth. "I'm gonna go to the bathroom."

"Must be a nervous stomach," Freckles said when Trina was out of earshot. "I got like that after I met my fourth husband. The man would barely look at me and my tummy would get to churning and I'd have to make a beeline for the nearest ladies' room."

Ethan's brow shot up to his hairline at Freckles's revelation of information nobody needed to hear. But he was quick to recover when he leaned forward, peering up at Monica. "Uh…the other reason I brought her in for breakfast this morning was because I was hoping you could give her some sort of pep talk?"

"Me? I'm not quite sure what I could say to make her any less nervous. I hated school, too."

"Really?" Ethan asked, his gaze traveling down the front of her and back up again. "But you're so smart. I assumed you were one of those teacher's pet types who would get straight As and be the president of the honor society and the French club and everything."

When he looked at her like that, Monica's own tummy began to flutter. "Well the straight As part is accurate, but joining any sort of society, even an academic one, would mean that I'd have to be social. And socializing isn't exactly my thing. Obviously, kids need school, but deep down I don't blame Trina for just wanting to hang out at the library and read."

Trina voluntarily returned from the restroom after only a couple of minutes—which was a vast improve-

ment from the last time she'd been in the café and had
gone there to hide—and Monica took their orders. There
weren't many people in the restaurant this morning and,
normally, Freckles would've been leaning against their
table, chatting up a newcomer like Trina. But the owner
was conspicuously busy visiting with Scooter and Jonesy,
who were practically permanent fixtures in the restaurant. What was odder was the fact that Freckles kept her
normally loud and joyful voice hushed and would cast occasional glances toward Ethan and Trina whenever they
weren't looking.

Freckles didn't leave the old cowboys' booth until
Ethan was paying his check, which was right about when
Monica saw the angle of the woman's bright magenta-
tinted grin and realized she was up to something.

"You know, sugar, it's such a slow morning," Freckles
said to Monica as though an idea had just occurred to her
and hadn't been percolating in her over-teased and heav-
ily hair-sprayed head this whole time. Putting an orange-
spandex-covered hip on the edge of the counter near the
cash register, her boss continued. "Plus, you're already
familiar with all the teachers and half of the kids over
at that school. Why don't you take off early and go with
Ethan and Trina, to ease her into her first day?"

His daughter's face lit up and it suddenly occurred to
Monica that she was becoming a little too ingrained in the
father-daughter-bonding experience. And Freckles was
becoming a little too ingrained in the matchmaking-her-
employees experience.

Monica didn't want to overshadow Ethan's role or in
any way interfere with them getting to know each other
better. "I doubt I'd be all that helpful. Besides, isn't the

first day of school one of those big milestones that should be just the two of you?"

"Just the two of us and the other couple of hundred parents and kids at drop-off," Ethan murmured before turning to Trina and leaning down. "What would make you feel the most comfortable?"

"I'd like Monica to come with us." Trina's voice was barely over a whisper, as all the other customers around them had gotten quieter so they could overhear the sidebar conversation. "And then after school, you and me can still get ice cream at Noodie's for our milestone, whatever that is."

"Sounds like a plan to me," Ethan replied, then rose back to his full height. "As long as Monica is okay with it."

"Please?" the girl asked, the earnestness in her clear blue eyes making Monica's rib cage squeeze against her heart. She didn't know who looked more hopeful—Trina or Ethan.

"I'd really owe you." Ethan's pleading smile made her knees wobble. "Again."

That's right. She was already ahead of him in the favors department. It took every ounce of restraint not to think about Ethan's text message last night. She'd had to turn off her phone to keep from asking where he needed to go that he couldn't take a child. Since it would be after dark, she doubted it was to a work site, which only left one other explanation. Ethan had a date. With another woman.

Which was why she needed to make it clear that she would only do favors that benefitted Trina—not Ethan. A few minutes later, when he held open the truck door for her, she told him as much.

"I'm only doing this because Trina could use the moral

support." Monica shot a glance into the backseat before fixing Ethan with her most serious look. "Next time, when it comes to making your life easier, you're on your own."

Ethan offered his hand to Trina as they walked across the parking lot of the elementary school, but his daughter didn't take it. Instead, he was forced to jam his fists into his coat pockets as if he hadn't just been completely rejected by an eleven-year-old.

Yeah, she was probably too old for holding hands. She did, however, stay pretty glued to his side so he should be thankful that the girl didn't find him totally repulsive.

Monica waved to the crossing guard and several other parents who stood on the front steps of Sugar Falls Elementary School watching them approach. Trina scooted even closer to him to the point that half of her thin body was hidden behind him. Ethan's instinct was to shield her from danger, but Carmen Gregson approached wearing her full police uniform and towing two identical nine-year-old boys behind her. Ethan was eager to ask the woman if she'd been in touch with Trina's caseworker back in Texas. But with so many eyes on them, he should probably wait until after school drop-off.

"Hey, Miss Alvarez," one of the Gregson twins (he could never remember which one was Aiden and which one was Caden) ran up to Monica after twisting out of his mom's hand. "Did you get any more of those pirate detective books in yet?"

"I'm expecting a shipment today. Maybe you can come by the library later this afternoon with my friend Trina. She's new to the school."

"Are you Trina?" the other twin asked.

His daughter moved even farther behind him, her

beanie-covered head peeking out from around his bicep. So she was nervous, but at least she was curious.

Ethan loosely wrapped his arm around her shoulder, but allowed her to stay pressed close to his hip. "This is my daughter, Trina Renault. Trina, these two rascals are Aiden and Caden Gregson and they're in…uh, third grade?"

"Fourth," the pair corrected him in unison, as if Ethan should have any idea of which grades went with which age group.

"I'm in fifth," Trina's voice was faint, but at least she was talking and not running straight for the girls' room.

"That's Mr. Yasikochi's class," Caden, or possibly Aiden, replied. Ethan really should know how to tell his best friend's kids apart by now. "He's the coolest teacher here. During our last assembly, he challenged the principal and the rest of the teachers to a spelling bee and now all the students get to pick which words they gotta spell. The winner's class gets a pudding cup party."

"Do you like pudding cups?" Aiden, or possibly Caden, asked.

"I guess," Trina replied.

"Come with us," one of the twins said, pulling on her jacket sleeve. "We'll show you where the cafeteria is and where we line up after recess and where the PE teacher keeps the best dodge balls locked in her office and where…"

The boys' voices faded as they pulled a taller Trina between them and peppered her with an overload of information. When they got to the top of the steps, she looked back at Ethan, her eyes wide and uncertain.

"Go ahead, Trina," Ethan said, capturing Monica's hand to pull her along. "We'll be right behind you."

Monica made a slight squeak and her head did a double take at his fingers resting against hers. But Ethan liked having her close, he wasn't about to let go. Besides, with all the kids darting in every which direction, he didn't want to accidentally get separated from her in all this chaos. Her cheeks turned a rosy shade of pink and several of the other parents murmured to each other on the steps as she took quick tiny steps to keep up with his bigger strides.

As soon as they set foot inside the building, Ethan was hit with the scent of glue and pencil lead and industrial-strength cleaner. Apparently not much had changed in over twenty years. This place smelled exactly like every elementary school he'd ever attended. And with his father's job that required them to move every eighteen months or so, Ethan was an expert.

A shrill bell sounded, making Ethan flinch. Maybe they couldn't do anything about the aroma, yet one would think they would've developed a more pleasant ringtone by now. Man, he was glad he didn't have to stay. If hating school was a genetic trait, poor Trina must've inherited it from him.

Kids scattered in all directions—including their nine-year-old tour guides, who promised to see Trina on the playground at recess—and Monica and Ethan were left standing alone in the hallway with his daughter.

Ethan had logged at least twenty parachute maneuvers, along with countless rescue and recon missions by both land and sea into enemy territory. Yet, he'd never experienced the type of paralyzing confusion as he did right that second in the hallway of an American elementary school. Well, except for last Saturday at the mall. And the Wednesday before that when Trina arrived on his doorstep. Hell, was this constant fish-out-of-water feeling *ever* going to cease?

Thank goodness for Monica, their undesignated team leader who'd managed to wiggle away from Ethan's grasp a few minutes ago when a couple of moms cornered him about attending the next PTA meeting.

"Let's go to the front office and meet Principal Cromartie." Monica smiled at Trina while Ethan didn't get so much as a passing glance. "He usually likes to walk new students to their classrooms."

"That's right," Ethan said, recalling the principal saying as much when they'd been here last Friday to register. At the time, he'd felt as though he was signing his life away with all those forms and permission slips the admissions clerk had shoved in front of him.

Compared to all the hoops they'd had to jump through a few days ago, this morning's meeting with the principal seemed almost anticlimatic. Dr. Cromartie's skin was smooth enough to make the thin, lanky African American man appear to be in his forties, but the shock of white, wiry hair on top of his head had Ethan thinking the head of the school was much older. Either way, the gentleman had a commanding presence and spoke confidently to Trina about how well she would do in Mr. Yasikochi's class, then asked Ethan and Monica to stay outside and wait for him as he opened a door with a hand-painted sign that read *Learning is Great in Room #8.*

"Have a good day," Monica said to Trina, who was already looking at the ground.

"Remember, I'll be standing outside on the steps at three o'clock," Ethan offered what reassurance he could. They'd gone over the day's schedule several more times last night and twice this morning. "And then we'll go get ice cream."

He was hoping for at least a nod, but his daughter surprised him by lifting her face and staring right at him as she spoke. "Don't forget that I'm also going to Monica's for dinner so that you can go to your meeting."

"I won't forget," he said, lifting his hand in a wave that probably came across as way too upbeat. Trina's own hand flicked upward, but her wave wasn't even half as enthusiastic.

When the classroom door closed behind his daughter and the principal, Monica turned to him. "You have a meeting tonight?"

"Yeah." He rocked back on his heels and glanced down the hall toward the exit door. Man, it was warm in this hallway.

"What kind of meeting?"

Ethan peeled off his coat and was stuck having to loop it through his arm. He wanted to reply, *The kind that's anonymous.* But after seeing Monica's facial reaction to Trina's comment about Chantal using "medicine" to stay skinny, he didn't know if he was ready for her to judge him the same way. Before Trina, he wouldn't have had a problem answering the question. Now, however, he flashed back to the insinuation Monica had made last week in the kitchen of the Cowgirl Up Café when she'd all but accused him of being a deadbeat dad. Since then, there might've been a slight thawing in her opinion of him, but he wasn't ready to find out. Instead he shrugged as if it was no big deal. "The kind that's personal."

She lowered her eyelids skeptically. "Sounds like a date to me."

"Would you be jealous if it was a date?" He wiggled

his eyebrows while trying to tamp down the thread of hope that began to coil in his belly. If she was jealous, that meant she cared. About him.

"Not a chance." Her response would've been more believable if she hadn't added a frustrated little huff afterward.

"I think you would be." He leaned in closer, letting his eyes drop to her full mouth as she opened and closed her lips several times. However, before she could utter so much as a denial, Dr. Cromartie walked back out into the hallway to join them.

"Thanks for waiting for me," the principal said. "Would you mind coming into my office?"

The older gentleman didn't wait for a response, walking away like a man accustomed to students following him.

"Oh... I'm sure you don't need me—" Monica started, but Ethan's hand immediately found hers again and he steered them toward the front of the school.

"We came in the same car, remember?" he murmured under his breath. Plus, he wasn't about to let her off the hook so easily. If she was going to start a conversation about the subject of dating, then he would sure as hell finish it.

The smooth skin against her jaw tightened, but Monica refused to meet his gaze, stiffly allowing him to lead her into Dr. Cromartie's office.

"So we got Trina's file from her prior school," the principal said as he gestured for them to take a seat. The older man picked up a blue folder and perched on the edge of his desk. "It's not completely comprehensive because her attendance was pretty spotty the past couple of years."

"I figured as much," Ethan replied, hoping Dr.

Cromartie wasn't judging him for being the flaky parent who hadn't made her go to school. Of course, his excuse of not being in his daughter's life before now didn't exactly make him an award-winning dad either.

"According to her grades and state testing results, her grammar and language scores are off the charts. So she's a very smart girl."

Ethan sat up a little straighter, pride filling his chest at an accomplishment that didn't technically belong to him. This might actually be the first time he'd ever been in a principal's office and not gotten a stern lecture.

"However...?" Monica pressed, ruining Ethan's short-lived moment of smugness.

"However," Dr. Cromartie gave a brief nod. "When she was in third grade, one of her teachers identified Trina as having dyscalculia."

Monica made a murmuring noise and Ethan looked between the only two people in the room with college degrees. "What does dyscalcu...whatever it's called. What does that mean?"

"Dyscalculia is a developmental disorder that makes it difficult to comprehend numbers and understand math concepts. For example, someone with dyscalculia might not remember which order numbers go in, or they struggle to identify the difference between a plus sign and a minus sign. Oftentimes, people refer to it as math dyslexia."

"That explains why she was pretty adamant about not going to school," Monica offered, putting a hand on Ethan's shoulder as though she was offering him comfort. "She's been struggling in math."

As much as he enjoyed the warmth of her touch, he didn't exactly need to be consoled. In fact, his back sagged against the seat in relief. "That's great."

"I'm sorry?" Dr. Cromartie pulled his chin back. "Are you saying that you're happy about this diagnosis?"

"Well, not happy. I mean, I'm definitely *un*happy about the fact that she struggled for so long and that she never got the help she needed. I'm downright pissed that she's had to go through this and so much more without me being there to support her. But I'm relieved that we're getting some answers and that we can get her on track now. You already said she was smart, right?" Ethan asked and waited for Dr. Cromartie's slow nod of assent. "Then this math dyslexia is the only thing wrong with Trina."

"I don't know if I would characterize it as something being *wrong* with her," Monica started.

"No, of course not. I just meant that if we have an explanation for why her brain does what it does, then we can get busy and fix it."

"Well, like dyslexia, it isn't necessarily curable," Dr. Cromartie warned. "But there are specialized tutoring and strategies that can help a person overcome it."

"Great." Ethan smacked his hands together. "How do we sign her up for that class?"

"As a smaller school, we don't exactly have a budget for specialty programs like that here. There are schools in Boise that could better accommodate this sort of—"

Ethan braced his palms on his knees. "I'm not moving her. No way. She's already been through too much and I don't think it would be fair to make her start somewhere new again."

Okay, so he wasn't just looking out for Trina's best interests in that regard. He also preferred not to uproot himself when he was just getting settled and had developed a dependable support system. Just like on the airplanes when they tell people to put on their own oxygen masks before helping others, Ethan's personal self-care would be essential if he truly wanted to be a better parent for his daughter. Really, it'd be better for *both* of them if they could avoid having any more disruptions in their lives.

"We have after-school tutors who come into the library a few days a week," Monica offered, placing a calming hand on top of his twitching fingers. "I can ask around to see if there's someone who specializes in dyscalculia. But you'd probably have to pay them out of pocket."

He studied the woman who sat beside him, the woman who was consistently a source of quiet strength and seemed to always know the answers before he could even think of the questions. He flipped his palm over, lacing his fingers through hers and giving them an instinctive squeeze in appreciation. God, it felt good not to be sitting here alone.

"I might not be rich, but I'll spend every damn dime on Trina's education if that's what it takes to get her where she needs to be. Maybe it didn't matter to Chantal, but it does to me. I want to help her the best way I can." He smiled gratefully at Monica, and looked back at Dr. Cromartie. "We'll start working on this as soon as we find the right tutor."

It also meant that Ethan would be spending a lot more time at the library.

Chapter Seven

"Hey, Monica," Nurse Dunn called, poking her head out of the health office. The woman wore medical scrubs covered with teddy bears and carried a coffee mug stamped with two different shades of lipstick. "Were you talking to Dr. Cromartie about the open school librarian position?"

"Um..." Monica tried not to look at Ethan behind her or in any way signal that they'd just been in the principal's office together. "No. We were just going over some tutoring programs at the city library."

"Oh." Nurse Dunn's eyes landed on Ethan's hand which had somehow nestled its way into Monica's again. The first time they'd held hands had been so they could stay together as they fought traffic in the crowded hallway. Then, in the office, the gesture had been more of a show of emotional support between friends. Now, though, his firm, wide grip was a little more difficult to write off as platonic. In fact, she didn't know what burned more—the area just below her wrist where his thumb was tracing slow, steady circles, or her cheeks that were flaming with mortification. "Well, if you know anyone who is interested, send them our way."

"I will," Monica replied, but it came out in a muffle and she had to clear her throat to repeat herself.

She stepped into the hallway, hoping that the quicker she walked, the easier it would be to dislodge Ethan's hand. But the man wasn't letting go. Obviously, she could yank hers away, however, that would only serve as an admission that his touch had any sort of effect on her. So she kept her spine stiff and her head facing forward and tried to pretend that she hadn't even noticed how overwhelming, yet natural, it felt to have his long, work-roughened fingers settled against hers.

There'd been such a suffocating warmth in the school hallway that Monica sucked in deep gulps of the cold February air when they got outside. She should've steeled herself better for the sudden drop in temperature, though, because her shoulders let out an uncontrollable shiver, causing Ethan to release her hand so that he could wrap that arm around her waist and pull her toward him.

His body shielded the wind from her and it was tough not to notice how perfectly she fit against him.

Okay. She'd only allow herself to enjoy the strength and warmth of his protective arm for a few more steps. But before they could make it past the sidewalk, Carmen caught up with them in the parking lot.

"My boys forgot these in the back of my squad car. I swear if their heads weren't attached, they'd forget those, too." She held up two lunch boxes—one Batman and one Spider-Man. "Anyway, I'm glad I caught you guys alone."

Monica opened her mouth to argue that despite the way she was pressed up to his side, she and Ethan weren't really alone. At least not like *that*. And not on purpose. However, Carmen didn't bat an eye as she continued, "I got a call from Trina's caseworker this morning."

"What did they say?" Ethan stiffened beside her, but didn't let go. Monica could only imagine the type of information he would need to brace himself for. Her own muscles were probably equally as tense at that moment.

"She reiterated pretty much what Trina already told you. Chantal DeVecchio has had numerous arrests for drug-related charges. Irene DeVecchio, Trina's grandmother, primarily raised her seeing as how Chantal was in and out of jail and rehab so often. The Texas Department of Family and Protective Services didn't open the case until Irene's health began to decline and Trina's school attendance suffered. The caseworker was assigned primarily to help with social services and to watch over the situation and make reports. She'd even referred them to family court to get Trina's guardianship legally established and to look into the possibility of other relatives raising the girl if and when Irene could no longer do so. She said your name came up when Trina asked her to do a search for her father."

"Trina mentioned that she'd been the one to find me, not her mom." Ethan lifted his face toward the cloudless sky, but his eyes were squeezed shut and his hand slipped from her waist to find hers once again—as if he was dizzy and Monica was the only thing grounding him. "I wanted to ask her more about that, but she shuts down if I try to get too much information from her at once."

"The caseworker said that when Irene passed away, Chantal took off with Trina and they stayed off the radar for a while. She was relieved when I told her that the girl was here with you."

"Does that mean they'll let her stay with me?" Ethan's normally unexpressive eyes were flooded with determination and resolve. She'd seen him friendly, she'd seen him charming, she'd even seen him confused. But this was the second time this morning she'd witnessed his intensity when it came to Trina's well-being. Maybe he was truly serious about wanting his daughter, after all.

Carmen's expression was a bit more guarded. "Texas is referring the case to the authorities here in Idaho. They'll be in contact with you soon to set up a home visit."

"A home visit for what?"

"To make sure that you're providing Trina with suitable living conditions and to probably interview you both to determine if being in your custody is in her best interest."

Ethan let out a whooshing breath, his shoulders relaxing. "What do you think, Carmen? You think I can pass the home visit so that they'll let me keep her?"

"My personal opinion? Of course they will. My professional opinion, however, is that you never know what can happen in these kinds of situations. Like I told you last week, it might be beneficial to retain an attorney, just to make sure all the legalities are in order."

Ethan nodded, then looked at Monica. "What about you, Mon? If you were the caseworker, would you let me keep her?"

Her tummy quivered at his use of the intimate nickname again and her body grew warm at the realization that he craved her reassurance. If he'd asked her to direct him to the family law treatises or the top-rated parenting books, it'd be no problem. Yet, here in the real world—away from the reference desk—she would only be offering him false hope.

Before she could say as much, the phone in the back pocket of her jeans vibrated.

"Excuse me for a sec," she said, stepping away to answer the call from an unknown number. "Hello?"

"Hey, Monica, this is Marcia over at Duncan's Market." Marcia only stopped in the library once a year or so to browse the self-help books, yet always left empty-handed. She'd also been a few years ahead of Monica in high school and even back then was well established as one of the most notorious gossips in town.

"Hi, Marcia. What can I do for you?" Scrunching her nose, Monica thought, *Please let this phone call be about the Motivational Mondays book club and not about why Monica has been spending so much time lately with Ethan Renault.*

"The reason I'm calling is because your grandmother came in this morning to do some shopping, but when she got to the checkout line, she didn't seem to have her purse."

A knot of dread formed in the pit of Monica's stomach. "Is she still there?"

"She is. She got pretty agitated so Mauricio, our deli manager, took her into the back office to talk about rotisserie chicken recipes. I think it's calming her down, but you should probably swing by and pick her up."

Ethan approached, his dark brow lifted in a silent question. Monica covered the mouthpiece of the phone and whispered, "Gran's over at the market. I have to go get her."

He nodded, so Monica removed her hand to speak

into the phone just as Ethan added, "Tell them we're on our way."

Marcia gasped on the other end. "Oh my. Is that a man I just heard in the background?"

Monica's cheeks flooded with heat and she squeaked out, "I'll be right there."

Ethan drove Monica straight to Duncan's Market and, despite the fact that she insisted he leave her there, he followed her into the store. "Your car is still at the café and I don't have to be on the job site until ten o'clock. So unless you want your gran walking to your car in her bathrobe and tap shoes, you should probably let me give you guys a ride."

"But then Marcia Duncan is going to know that we were together this morning," Monica said through clenched teeth as she forced a smile and a wave at one of the cashiers.

"It's Sugar Falls and all the parents and teachers just saw us at the elementary school together." He glanced down at the titanium chronograph watch the guys in his platoon gave him for setting a record on the combat diver qualifications course. "I'm sure Marcia, as well as the rest of the five thousand people who live within the city limits, already know you were with me. In fact, they've probably been speculating on it for at least a good hour by now."

"Oh hey there, Ethan," Marcia greeted them in the same syrupy tone she'd used when she'd followed him and Trina around the store last week, pointing out all the specials while not-so-subtly throwing in a leading question. *We have strawberry Pop-Tarts on sale. Do you have strawberry Pop-Tarts back in...where are you from again, dear?* As they'd stocked up on groceries, Marcia had tried to stock up on gossip about the person everyone else in town was referring to as his secret daughter. "I thought I recognized your voice when I was on the phone with Monica, but I knew she'd already left the café to go to… where were you guys so early this morning?"

See, Ethan shot Monica a knowing look, but her head was on a swivel—probably scanning the store for her wayward grandmother—and didn't seem to register anything else. Not wanting to give in to Marcia's blatant attempts to fish for information, he asked, "Is Mrs. Alvarez still here?"

"She's back here. Mauricio is trying to keep her calm by letting her chop up cabbage for coleslaw, but she refuses to wear the disposable gloves or put her hair up in the hairnet. So we won't be able to sell any of it."

"There you are, *mija*," Gran said to Monica when they entered the deli prep kitchen. "And you brought your handsome friend with you again."

"Hi, Gran." Monica's tone was laced with caution. He recognized it as the same one he used when he wanted to ask Trina a question and didn't want to scare her off. "We stopped by to give you a ride home. You remember *Mr. Renault*, don't you?"

Ethan would've laughed at the way Monica emphasized his formal name, as if that would lead Marcia—or anyone else—to think there wasn't anything casual going on between them. But now wasn't the time to be teasing her about the status of their relationship. Not only because her grandmother was possibly in a delicate mental state, but also because he wasn't exactly sure of the definition of their relationship at that point.

"Of course I remember you, Ethan," Gran replied, then

winked at the store owner. "He spends quite a bit of time at our house, you know."

Monica's cheeks turned a charming shade of crimson. "That was back in November when he was working on our kitchen, Gran."

"And he stayed over very late after he brought you home the other night, *mija*."

"Oh my." Marcia's eyes couldn't get any rounder and her mouth hung open like one of those bottom-feeding catfish hanging out at the Lake Rush docks waiting for someone to drop a tasty morsel their way.

Ethan's fingers twitched. "Mrs. Alvarez, if you're all done here, why don't we head on back to your place and maybe you can make me something for lunch?"

Really, he wasn't very hungry after adding that cinnamon roll to his normal breakfast earlier. Plus, it wasn't exactly lunchtime, but when they'd worked on her house, the older woman had seemed to enjoy plying him and Kane with homemade food no matter what time of day it was.

"For you, *mijo*, I'll make some fresh *conchas* and that Mexican hot chocolate you like," Gran said, using the masculine version of the endearment she usually reserved for her granddaughter. "But I'll have to stop at the market on the way home and pick up some things."

Monica's breath came out in a sigh. "Gran, we're at the market right now."

"Oh, well then that's convenient." The woman took off the service deli apron someone had given her, revealing the shabby bathrobe she'd been wearing underneath. Her feet gave off a musical ping with each step as she walked across the tile floor. She looped her frail arm through Monica's, stifling a yawn. "*Mija*, go grab us a cart so we can do our shopping."

"Um, Mrs. Alvarez—" Marcia lifted her plump fingers in a small wave "—you still have your cart of groceries over by the register. Remember, you told us not to put anything back until Monica got here with your purse."

Monica patted her jacket pockets. "That might be an issue. I left my own purse at the café when I took off with Ethan this morning."

"So then you want me to put the groceries in the cart away?" Marcia scratched the frizzy blond hair on top of her head. "All of them?"

"*Donde estan, mija?*" Mrs. Alvarez's face grew pinched. "*Donde esta la comida que acabo de compare? Y por que me esta viendo asi la gorda?*"

Ethan had to rely on some of the Spanish phrases he'd learned back when he'd been stationed in San Diego near the border. But he understood enough to know that the older woman had just taken a turn and didn't know where they were or what had happened to the food she'd just bought. She'd also made an unflattering remark about Marcia Duncan's size, judging by the tight grin Mauricio Norte was trying to hide and the shushing sounds Monica was making at her.

Ethan fished the keys out of his pocket and handed them to Monica. "Why don't you take Gran to the truck and I'll pay for the groceries?"

"Come on," Marcia said, casting a narrowed look at Mrs. Alvarez who was now speaking in rapid-fire Spanish. "We already scanned everything and have it bagged up front."

Ethan followed the owner of the market to the cash register and didn't even ask what was in the two shopping carts. He just wanted to get out of there and get Monica and her grandmother home.

When he got to the parking lot, Gran was already in the backseat. Her lips were moving, but no sound came out as she slouched against the armrest and stared vacantly out the window.

"Oh my gosh," Monica said when she saw all the bags in the two carts he towed behind him. "Why in the world was she buying so much food? I don't even want to know how much money I owe you for all that."

Ethan was glad he'd crumpled up the receipt and shoved it deep into his coat pocket on the way outside. He doubted Monica had an extra two hundred dollars lying around to pay him back. Not that he'd let her.

"We can figure all that out later." Ethan jerked his head toward the cab of his truck. "How's she doing?"

"Exhausted." Monica reached into one of the carts to haul out a paper bag. "Every time she has an episode it takes a lot out of her, physically."

Ethan lowered his tailgate and, when he took the bag of groceries from her, the backs of his fingers inadvertently grazed the underside of her breast. A current of electricity shot through his body and he dropped the bag, making a loud *thunk* against the metal shopping cart.

He'd touched women before. Hell, he'd even touched Monica before and they'd pretty much been holding hands at the school all morning. But that was more out of necessity. Sort of. It was also before Marcia Duncan made it a point to suggest that their relationship was more than just friendship.

Now, though, it was different since they were both aware of their attraction and this time the accidental contact through her wool coat sent waves up one of his arms and down the other. The blush rising over her neck told him that she'd felt the same sensation. In fact, Monica refused to look at him as they finished loading the rest of the bags into the truck, which was a sure sign that his touch had equally affected her.

And that made him feel pretty damn good.

Their house was only a mile away from the store, yet Gran was lightly snoring by the time Ethan pulled into the driveway. Monica turned around in her seat to wake her grandmother, but Ethan put his finger to his mouth. "Let her sleep. I can carry her upstairs."

Seeing her tiny and frail grandmother cradled in Ethan's arms would have been touching if it hadn't reminded Monica of the way someone would carry a child. It broke Monica's heart to sit back and watch such a strong woman grow increasingly dependent with each passing day.

Leading the way to Gran's bedroom, Monica pulled the quilted cover back so that he could get her sleeping grandmother settled on the bed. She reached down to unbuckle the strap of Gran's tap shoe and gasped at the maroon-colored bruise on the papery thin skin underneath.

"Looks like a blood blister," Ethan whispered. "How do you think it happened?"

"Hard to say. She usually gets them just by bumping into something. But the rest of her feet are all purplish and raw—like she maybe walked all the way to the store."

Monica's car was still at the café and most of the nearby neighbors knew better than to give her grandmother a ride when she was dressed like this. Thankfully, some of her neighbors tended to stop by and check in on Gran because they knew Monica couldn't afford a full-time caregiver when she was at work. She never would've been able to manage it without all the added help. Although, she had to wonder if she was managing anything anymore.

"Do you need me to help up here or should I bring the groceries in?" Ethan's fingers quivered slightly before he shoved them in his pockets.

The guy was definitely itching to get out of here. Not that she could blame him. To an outsider, Gran's behavior must seem totally crazy. "If you could just set the bags on the front porch, I'll get them from there."

Just like two days ago, Monica carefully repacked the dance shoes in their box and pulled the quilt up over her grandmother. Also, just like two days ago, when she returned downstairs, she found Ethan in her kitchen—his coat tossed over a chair as he put three cartons of eggs in the refrigerator.

He glanced at her when she entered, but didn't stop what he was doing. "I wasn't sure where everything went, so I guessed. The good news is that you won't be running out of pickles anytime soon."

He nodded toward the open pantry cabinet with an entire shelf dedicated to duplicate jars of the same dill variety and Monica sighed. "Gran is always afraid of running out of certain things. The crazy thing is that she doesn't even like pickles, so they just sit there until I can go through and sneak a few containers out at a time. Same thing with the diet root beer and the grape jelly. I'm worried that the people who run the canned food drives are going to ask me to stop donating so often."

"That explains the stash of Oreos I found hidden on the top shelf."

"Actually, those are mine. Gran thinks store-bought cookies are a sin, but I lived on them during finals week at college and now, anytime I'm stressed, it's like my body craves them."

"I'm guessing you're stressed pretty often?" Ethan lifted two five-pound bags of rice and she tried not to stare at the way it made the muscles under his snug thermal T-shirt stretch.

"Some days—like today—are a little rougher than others."

He paused. "Maybe I shouldn't bring Trina over tonight, after all?"

"No, Gran'll be up and at 'em in a couple of hours. Usually, when she wakes up after having an episode, it's like a reboot. You know how if you get too many windows running on your computer, you can shut it off and then restart it to get it working faster?" Monica waited for Ethan's slow nod. "That's what her brain does. So she'll most likely remember that Trina is coming tonight and will want to make something special for dinner. It's probably why she went to the store in the first place."

"Well, I wouldn't want to disappoint Gran." Ethan's smile was back and Monica's knees went as soft as the fresh loaf of white bread in her hands. "But I don't want it to be any extra work for you."

"Actually, Trina will be a positive distraction for Gran. Really, it'd be helping me to have her over. Besides, who else is going to eat all this food?"

They worked in silence emptying the rest of the bags. When they finished, Ethan lifted both of his arms over his head to stretch, causing the hem of his shirt to rise and reveal a strip of smooth, chiseled skin just above his belt line.

Monica's mouth went dry and her head went a little

fuzzy as she imagined what it would be like to undo the first button on his fly.

Oh boy. She really needed to get him out of her house before her imagination led her down a dangerous path. Forcing herself to swallow, she asked, "Shouldn't you be heading back to work now?"

He looked at the heavy-duty watch on his wrist. "Probably. Are you going to stay here to watch your grandmother or do you need a lift back to your car?"

Monica groaned as she sank into one of the dining room chairs. "I can't afford to miss any more work. Let me call one of our neighbors and see if they can come over and check on her a few times."

Mr. Simon had recently retired and Monica pulled out her cell phone to call him while Ethan sent his own boss a text.

After hanging up, she ran upstairs to change out of her boots and Cowgirl Up T-shirt and into something more appropriate for the library. She checked on Gran one more time, planting a soft kiss on the older woman's spotted cheek before switching on the long-range baby monitor they'd purchased a few months ago.

Monica asked Ethan to lock up as she navigated across the snowy grass as quickly as her narrow pencil skirt would allow. Mr. Simon was already on his own porch to take the monitor's walkie-talkie unit so he could listen to Gran while he was working in his garage.

"That Ethan Renault?" Mr. Simon asked, nodding toward Ethan's truck.

"Oh. Um, yes. He's giving me a ride back to the café to get my car."

"Your gran tells us you're spending a lot of time with him lately." Mr. Simon was nice enough, but he tended to read a few too many true crime stories and was suspicious of anyone he hadn't known for at least twenty years.

"I wouldn't say *a lot*…"

"Heard you went down to Boise with him to go shopping."

"News travels fast." *As usual*, Monica wanted to add. "But did you also hear we went with his eleven-year-old daughter?"

"Might've heard something about that. My wife thinks he's in the market for a new mom for his little girl. But I told Deb that everyone in town knows he was interested in you long before the child showed up—"

"Okay, well I better get going, Mr. Simon. Call me when Gran wakes up."

When Monica climbed into Ethan's truck, her fingers fumbled with the seat belt buckle as she kept replaying Mr. Simon's words about everyone thinking Ethan was interested in her. Her neighbor, though, was also a known conspiracy theorist who'd once questioned whether the government could listen in on the baby monitor, so she shouldn't give his illogical opinion another thought.

"Here," Ethan said, putting his hand over hers. Her skin hummed to life, just like it had when he'd accidentally brushed against her breast in the parking lot at the market. And when he'd spontaneously grabbed her hand for reassurance in the elementary school hallway before that. He snapped the metal mechanism into place, allowing his thumb to trace over hers afterward. "It can be tricky sometimes."

She stared at his tanned, callused fingers, mesmerized by the slow and gentle strokes he made against the ridge of her knuckle and all the way to her crescent-shaped nail.

Pull away, her brain told her.

Touch him back, her lower parts dared her.

Fortunately, her brain won out, but not until he'd made his way all the way to the tender flesh of her wrist. Her elbow hit the hard part of the glove box because she'd jerked her arm back so quickly.

He gave her a knowing smile, but instead of talking about what had just happened, Ethan thankfully put the truck in gear. When they turned onto Snowflake Boulevard, he asked, "How long do you think your gran will sleep?"

Monica shrugged, relieved they were talking about anything other than the way her body always responded to him. "It just depends on how bad the episode was. It's like her brain is working so hard to make sense of the world around her, that her body stops working in order to send all of the energy up there. Spanish is her first language, so when she reverts to it like she did earlier at the store, I know it's just a matter of time before she shuts down. I really appreciate the fact that you were there to drive us home."

"Pretty soon we're gonna need a scorecard to keep track of how many favors we owe each other."

"Maybe we shouldn't be keeping count of who owes who what." Or of how much time they were spending together. It was a slippery slope to be indebted to someone she was finding it harder and harder to resist. She squared her shoulders against the seat. "We're friends. That's what friends do. Help each other out."

"So that's all we are, huh?" he asked as he parked in front of the Cowgirl Up Café. "Friends?"

"Yep." She opened the door and jumped down from the cab before her eyes proved her mouth wrong. "I'm just your friend, Ethan."

"Well, that's more than we were a few weeks ago, so I guess we're making a little progress." His upper teeth did that thing where they scraped against his lower lip and she commanded her feet to move. But they ignored her and chose to obey him when he called out, "Hold on!"

Ethan opened his own door and, as he made his way around the truck, Monica gulped in enough cold air to fight the rising temperature inside her.

"You forgot this," he said, holding up the half apron she'd taken off on the way to Trina's school earlier. Before she could snatch it from him, he had already looped the strings around her back and was tying it just above her belly button. This time, though, when his fingers grazed against her torso she was positive that it was no accident. "And just for the record, my meeting tonight is not a date."

"And just for the record, it wouldn't be any of my business if it *was* a date." There, that sounded strong enough and almost believable. In fact, as she walked away, her knees grew steadier with each step until she almost believed it herself.

Chapter Eight

Ethan didn't realize how badly he'd needed to attend an AA meeting until he sat in that room at the community rec center on Monday night. Alcoholism could be a disease of loneliness and isolation—no matter how busy or social he was. Being with others who battled the same disease made Ethan feel a little less alone.

He and Commodore Russell were standing by the coffee machine in back when the older man removed the toothpick from his mouth and said, "You know what the Big Book says about shouldering the burdens and troubles of others?"

Ethan inhaled deeply and replied, "We find that we're soon overcome by them. But aren't Trina's burdens also my burdens?"

"Yep. But you don't want your burdens to become hers."

The old guy had a point. Ethan's sobriety was more important to him now than ever before. If that meant fortifying himself with more meetings, then that's what he'd do. Trina deserved to have him be the best father he could be.

However, he didn't want to overuse his goodwill with Monica—such as it might be—to ask her to keep babysitting Trina in the evenings. So before he left, he made a mental note to look into the AA sessions held during the day at Shadowview, the military hospital thirty minutes away.

Both Trina and Gran were yawning when he arrived at the Alvarez house to pick up his daughter and the gassy kitten. But neither one looked as exhausted as Monica. The circles under her eyes were faint, and her usually proud shoulders seemed to sag.

"How'd it go?" he asked her when she came out of the kitchen and met him in the entryway.

"Great. Gran taught Trina how to make flour tortillas and how to do Elvis's signature hip shake. Trina read some of her book to Gran and kept her from feeding Tootie too many black beans while I made a few phone calls. That reminds me, I lined up a math tutor to come to the library tomorrow. He's a graduate student down at Boise State, so he can only come on Tuesday and Thursday afternoons."

"You are incredible," he said, reaching out both of his arms in praise. Actually, his instinct had been to lift her up in a celebratory hug, but Ethan had stopped himself just in time. A pink flush crept up Monica's cheeks, perhaps from his compliment or perhaps because she knew that he'd been about to touch her again before he caught himself.

He hoped it was because she was also thinking about the last time he'd touched her and how *both* of their faces had filled with heat. Testing the waters, he softly placed a hand on her shoulder. "Seriously, Monica. I can't even begin to tell you how much I appreciate everything you've done for me these past few days."

Her indrawn gasp was as abrupt as her glance at his fingers. Yep. She was thinking about their physical attraction, too.

"Well, technically, I was doing it to help Trina," she said before dramatically lifting her own arms in a stretch as she yawned loudly. The move was probably intended to dislodge his hand, and it worked. Although, she probably didn't realize that it also caused a few of the buttons on her white blouse to gap, giving him a glimpse of a light pink lacy bra underneath. After a second yawn, she added, "But I'm also extremely grateful to you for helping me out at the market this morning."

Ethan lifted the corner of his mouth in a sly smile before repeating her own words. "Well, technically, I was doing it to help Gran. Although, I wouldn't be opposed to us helping each other—"

Monica's third and suspiciously fake yawn cut him off. "Whew. Sorry about that. It sure has been a long and interesting day."

"Then I don't want to keep you away from your bed." What Ethan really meant was that he wouldn't mind carrying her to bed himself. After briefly going upstairs earlier this morning, he'd found himself wondering about Monica's bedroom all afternoon. But with her grandmother and his daughter putting away Elvis records in the living room a few feet away, it wasn't as though he could just sweep the sleepy, sexy woman up into his arms. Instead, he cleared his throat and looked over his shoulder. "Come on, Tri, let's head home."

His daughter patted Mrs. Alvarez's hand, which was the biggest display of affection he'd witnessed from the child—at least to another human. She had plenty of affection for the bean-eating kitten.

"Come back again, soon," Mrs. Alvarez offered, and Monica didn't correct the older woman or otherwise appear to be put out.

Well, if Ethan had a clear shot, he was certainly going to take it. "Perhaps next Monday?" he suggested.

"Perfect," Mrs. Alvarez said while Monica just yawned. Probably too exhausted to protest.

The following morning, since Trina seemed to do best with a routine, Ethan took her to the Cowgirl Up Café again for breakfast, despite the fact that Monica was usually off on Tuesdays. On the way to school, they discussed the tutor and then confirmed their afternoon schedule at least three more times.

The same discussion took place every day that week and by Friday, he decided to drive down to Boise again to get Trina her own cell phone so she wouldn't have to stress about being forgotten at school.

"Text me or call me whenever you need to," he'd told her. And she did. Every day during her lunch break. At first, it was a passive reminder, such as "See u at 3." Then he began responding with memes of inspirational cat posters, such as the kitten with its paws attached to a window curtain and the slogan "Hang in there."

After a few days, she would write back "lol" or use a smiley face emoji, which was an improvement considering she still didn't smile that often in person.

By the second week of March, he honestly couldn't say that he'd gotten any more comfortable with his new role as Trina's primary caregiver, but they definitely had bonded over cat memes and had an established daily pattern that he could anticipate.

The mornings were still the easiest part of his day, even

though they were a bit rushed and consisted of cereal more often than made-to-order eggs at the Cowgirl Up Café. Swinging a hammer and climbing ladders on his various job sites gave him something physical he could focus on, although he was in serious need of anything a little more athletic.

He was always outside of the school at exactly three o'clock to pick up Trina, which would've been the highlight of his day if she didn't always look so miserable and defeated every time she came out the doors. Or if he could've avoided the other parents who were constantly trying to get him to bring two dozen treats for the bake sale or help organize the popcorn fund-raiser or chaperone the band field trip.

His daughter wasn't even in band.

Even the evenings weren't as difficult as he'd expected them to be, since he was usually busy not-burning (or sometimes phoning in) dinner while looking over Trina's homework or scratching his head at some of the characters on the YouTube videos she liked to watch. By the time he dropped in his rack at night to get some shut-eye, he was so mentally exhausted, sleep came easier than it ever had.

No, the biggest struggle for Ethan came in the late afternoons. "Happy hour time," he used to call it, back before any time of the day had become happy hour to him. He grew restless and antsy and even bored during that two-hour window when he transitioned from being a full-time working adult to being a full-time responsible parent. The worst was when Trina was at the library for tutoring on Tuesdays and Thursdays.

Ethan was left with absolutely nothing to do but sit in his truck and try not to think about drinking, or sit at a distant table in the library and try not to think about what

Monica would look like underneath her boxy cardigan sweaters and her stiff, button-up blouses.

That second Thursday afternoon in March, he'd finally decided to change into some workout clothes and go for a long-distance run while he waited for Trina. But he'd only made it a couple of miles when the rain began to pour down and—even though he'd run in much worse conditions than these—he turned back. He was soaking wet by the time he got to the library and thought about going home to change, but then he would've been late to pick up his daughter.

Walking in the library, Ethan's shoes squished and leaked water onto the old parquet floors. A mom whipped her head around, giving him the stink eye and putting her finger to her lips in the universal sign to be quiet. The old building was built in the late nineteenth century and, while it was both historical and unique, the architect apparently hadn't taken into account that the hexagon shape and open second-story floor plan only added to the acoustics and amplified every little peep.

His daughter was usually in one of the study rooms upstairs and there was no way to get there in these shoes without announcing his every step. Maybe he'd just find Monica instead and tell her to let Trina know he'd be a few minutes late.

"Hey," he said when he finally spotted the librarian in the hidden recesses of the nonfiction section, kneeling down near the lower shelf and passing a kid an oversize volume on frogs.

She dropped the book before the kid could take it, but the young boy didn't even notice because both pairs of eyes were on him.

"You're all wet, man," the boy stated the obvious, picking up his frog book and giving Ethan a gap-toothed grin before walking away.

Monica remained on her knees, though her lips parted and her glasses slipped down her nose as she aimed her gaze directly at his torso.

Extending his hand, he asked, "Do you need help getting up?"

"You're all wet," she said, not making any move to accept his offer or to otherwise rise to her feet. In fact, she continued to study him, making his skin heat under the cold, clinging fabric of his soaked shirt.

"So I've been told," he replied, his chest jutting out as though he was silently inviting her to look her fill.

"Your clothes are practically plastered to every muscle on your—"

The water trailing down his outstretched hand dripped onto her gray skirt, unfortunately drawing her attention from whatever it was she'd been about to say. But judging by the way her cheeks had gone crimson and her pupils had dilated, she didn't have to say anything. Monica was more than attracted to him, he realized with a satisfied smile. She was aroused.

She gave her head a little shake before putting her own palm in his. When he yanked her to her feet, he didn't release her. Rather, he used the momentum to pull her toward him. Monica put a hand on his chest, probably just to brace herself from getting any closer, and his heart hammered underneath her slender, delicate fingers.

"You're all wet." Monica knew she was repeating herself, but her dazed mind couldn't form any other thought as her pulse pounded in her ears.

"And *you're* all flushed," Ethan said with a smirk before leaning his wet face closer to hers. He stopped just short of kissing her, though, and her eyes darted down just in time to see his lips part ever so slightly in invitation.

Monica knew it was a mistake before she'd even risen up on her tiptoes. One minute she was looking for a book about the habitats of tree frogs and the next she had her lips planted all over a dripping wet Ethan Renault. She could taste the rain on his lips as her mouth slanted over his.

Her tongue was as eager as her hands that were gripping the damp fabric on his shoulders for leverage, pressing him up against the life science and zoology shelves. Or were those the foreign language shelves behind him? She didn't know and she no longer cared. All that mattered was that she'd finally let go of this attraction she'd been struggling to hold back for so long, and now she was making up for lost time.

His hands splayed around her lower back, just below her waist, as his tongue lazily stroked against hers. She was rushed and frenzied while he was slow and methodical, easing their kiss into a rhythm.

Reminding herself to breathe through her nose, she inhaled the salty, tangy scent of his skin and the familiar, musty smell of lignin from the books surrounding them. Kissing Ethan was like reading a fast-paced thriller set in a faraway land while being in the comfort of her own home. His mouth was a wild adventure, as exciting and thrilling as being on a roller coaster, while his steady arms were solid and reassuring, the safety bar keeping her in place as she enjoyed the ride.

Monica let her hands travel down his chest, exploring the hard peaks and ridged valleys of his muscles. His mouth trailed kisses across her jaw and she threw back her head, drawing in another ragged breath.

She was just slipping her fingers under the hem of his wet T-shirt when Ethan jumped away so quickly, his head thunked against the oak shelf behind him. Monica's initial instinct was to moan in disappointment. Yet, when she caught the panicked look in his eye, she nearly groaned in embarrassment for shocking him with her forwardness.

But the groan didn't come from Monica. It came from the eleven-year-old girl at the end of the aisle who'd just seen them.

Ethan didn't bother to say so much as a goodbye, let alone give Monica a proper thank-you. After all, what was there to say following a kiss like that?

He'd had to chase after Trina, who'd shot him a withering look before stomping toward the exit, her yellow backpack bouncing with each purposeful step as she broke out into a run in the parking lot. Luckily, the onslaught of rain must have discouraged her from taking off down the street, and she headed directly for his truck instead.

She was struggling with the door handle when he pulled up beside her to unlock the truck with his remote. He opened it for her, but couldn't even find the words to ask her what had her so upset. Not that his daughter was really one for coming out and discussing any uncomfortable feelings—a trait she'd probably inherited from him. Besides, Ethan had a feeling he already knew what was wrong. The problem was he didn't know how to fix the situation without making things worse.

While he'd never let uncertainty or poor planning prevent him from completing a mission before, fatherhood was proving to be the one assignment that left him in a constant state of doubt. At least when he'd been on deployments, he'd had the backing of his team and his squad leaders. Had his own dad ever felt this alone and confused? Feelings of ineptness filled Ethan as he climbed into the driver's seat.

He sighed as he put the key in the ignition, but before he could turn over the engine, Trina surprised him by saying, "Things were just starting to get normal. Why did you have to mess it all up by kissing *her*?"

In Ethan's defense, Monica had kissed *him* first. But since his daughter was showing some anger instead of the casual indifference she usually exhibited toward him, he wasn't about to miss an opportunity to find out what she was really thinking. Unfortunately, Trina's blue eyes had gone dark and stormy and glared at him with such accusation, he nearly winced.

Perhaps their standard operating procedure of mostly ignoring each other would've been preferable—just like remaining strapped into a perfectly good airplane would've been preferable to someone who was afraid of heights. But he was already at the free fall altitude and his parachute was packed with the rip cord in his hand. He had to make the jump.

Wiping the raindrops from his confused brow, he replied, "I thought you liked Monica."

Okay. Even he knew that sounded lame.

"I do." Trina crossed her arms and looked out the window.

"Well, I like Monica, too." He put his arm along the top of the bench seat as he turned to face her. It was also his way of letting her know that he wasn't going anywhere until they talked about why she was so upset.

"Sure you do. *For now.*"

He ran a hand through his wet hair as he exhaled. He'd heard that teenagers came equipped with plenty of sarcasm and attitude, but he'd hoped for a few more years of getting to know his daughter before he'd have to experience the full effects of adolescent hormones. "Trina, I'm trying to understand why you're upset. I really am. But I'm gonna need you to walk me through this."

"Chantal said that all men leave. But I was hoping that you would be different. Then again, you left us, too, so I don't see how."

Okay, so apparently this had something to do with her mother and him. That was just one more sin that Ethan was never going to live down. He could follow his twelve steps and try and make amends all he wanted, but some things were out of his hands. Circumstances were already too far gone and it wasn't fair for him to pretend that he could undo the past. He sighed and attempted a different approach.

"Tri, when I was younger, my mom told my dad she wanted a divorce."

"So your mom left you, too?" She lifted her lips into a quasi snarl. "That makes it okay for you to leave?"

"Not exactly. My parents shared custody of me. I was with my mom during the week and with my dad on the weekends. I hated it. So that Christmas, all I wanted from Santa was to have all of us back together in the same house."

"Only babies believe in Santa." She snorted, adding condescension to the current display of charming pre-teen attitude.

"Well, I was five," he replied a bit too defensively. Yep, ignoring each other would have definitely been preferable. Or perhaps he could've found a suitable cat meme for this situation.

His daughter waited a few beats then asked, "So I'm guessing they didn't get back together?"

"Nope. My mom died in a car crash with her new boy-friend on Christmas Eve."

Trina's face softened, but it wasn't his intent to garner

any sympathy points or to make this conversation about him. "What I'm trying to say is that I know what you're going through. It's normal for kids to hold out hope that their parents will eventually get back together."

"Wait. You think that I want you to get back together with Chantal?"

"Isn't that why you're mad at me for kissing Monica?"

"As if!" Trina rolled her eyes.

"Then why else wouldn't you want me to date her?"

Her brows shot up. "Are you guys dating?"

"Not formally."

"Exactly." Trina nodded as if everything was perfectly clear. However Ethan was more puzzled than before.

"Help me out here, Tri. Please."

"Chantal said that you left as soon as you got what you wanted from her."

"And what did she say I wanted from her?"

Trina shrugged. "I don't know. I guess the same thing as all those other men who came over but never took her out on dates. Kissing and gross stuff like that."

A chill went down Ethan's spine and a cold rage spread through his body. If Chantal knew what was best for her, she better stay long gone. Trina must've sensed the shift from his confusion to his disgust because she scooted closer toward the door, as if she needed to be ready to get away from him, too.

"I'm not mad," he lied to his daughter as he fought to unclench his hands. At least, he wasn't mad at *her.* "You can always tell me anything—say whatever is on your mind."

She studied him for several moments before taking a deep breath. "If you and Monica aren't dating and you're just kissing her, then that means you're gonna leave her, too."

Ethan closed his eyes and let his head fall back against the headrest. "So you *don't* want me to leave Monica?"

"No. I like her. And I like Gran."

"I like them, too, Tri. But just because we like somebody, doesn't mean that they'll like us back."

"You don't think Monica likes us?"

"Well, I know she likes *you*," he replied honestly. "She smiles a lot when you're around and she always has books set aside for you and she asks me how you're doing in school all the time."

"Hmm," Trina said, tilting her chin. "Maybe she likes you, too, then."

"Why do you think that?"

"Because last Monday night when we were eating, she asked about you."

Ethan's chest expanded. Now they were getting somewhere. "Oh yeah? What did she want to know about me?"

"She wanted to know if you were getting any better at making dinner. Then today, she told me she had a cookbook for you at the checkout desk. It's called *Crock Pot for Dummies*." Trina giggled at the last part.

"So that's two out of three," Ethan shrugged as though he didn't really care one way or the other. He knew better than to rely on a kid for matchmaking experience, but since he rarely got to engage in real conversations with his daughter, he convinced himself that he should ask more questions. "What about Monica smiling when I'm around?"

"Hmmm. It's more like a frown whenever you're talking to her. But when you're *not* talking to her, she does kinda stare at you. A lot."

"Wait. How does she stare at me?"

Trina grinned. "The same way she was looking at you after you kissed her."

Chapter Nine

The following Monday night, as he drove to the Alvarez house to pick up Trina after his meeting, Ethan thought about how he could get Monica alone, running through several scenarios in his mind. He needed to talk to her about that kiss between the library shelves last Thursday, mostly to explain why he'd left in such a hurry. While he hadn't been expecting it, he also hadn't been quite ready for it to end. In fact, who knew how far out of control things would've gotten if Trina hadn't interrupted them?

Thoughts of Monica's mouth against his had filled up his weekend to the point that he'd gone so stir-crazy being cooped up in his apartment, he'd needed a physical release. The weekends were usually his time to get outdoors and do something that fueled his adrenaline and reminded him that he was alive. Unfortunately, his choices in extreme sports were now somewhat limited with an eleven-year-old in tow.

It was still a bit too early in the season to get out on the rapids, so he couldn't take Trina white-water rafting. He'd tried to teach her how to snowboard on Saturday, but all the recent rain had made what little snow remained on the runs pretty icy and she'd given up after only two falls.

She'd been a good sport, though, asking to hang out in the lodge with the book she'd brought along so that he could spend an hour or so out on the slopes. They'd driven down to Boise on Sunday to try out an indoor rock climbing gym, but it wasn't the same as scaling up a granite cliff or, better yet, boulder jumping.

So by the time he pulled the truck in front of Monica's house, his nerves were humming with energy. Monica was already on the porch and he smiled at her apparent eagerness for his arrival.

Until he got closer and saw her face.

"What happened?" he asked as he crossed the front yard.

She was twisting a cloth towel in her hands. "I was in the kitchen doing dishes and didn't even hear them leave."

"Hear who leave?"

"Gran and Trina. They were in the living room listening to one of her Elvis records and then the needle started skipping. When I went in there to check on them, they were gone."

Gone. The word was a punch to Ethan's gut. "Maybe they went for a walk?"

Monica shook her head. "They took my car. I tried to call you, but it went straight to voice mail."

Ethan checked his phone. He'd turned off the ringer when he was at the meeting and forgot to switch it back on.

"Let's go find them," he said as he jogged to his truck.

"No, they're already on their way back. I called the police right away and Carmen found them at Noodie's getting ice cream. Here they are now."

A squad car turned onto the street and Ethan's stomach sank as if he'd swallowed a rock. He never wanted to see his child in the backseat of a police car again.

When he opened the door, Trina flew into his arms. "Shh, honey, it's okay," he told her as she clung to him.

Mrs. Alvarez's eyes were huge and her face was pale as Monica helped her out of the front seat.

"I don't know why I did that, *mija*." Gran handed Monica's purse to her, which was probably how the older woman had gotten the car keys.

"Oh, Gran," Monica said, pulling her into an embrace. "Are you okay?"

"Just a little shook up. We left your car at the ice cream shop. Officer Gregson wouldn't let me drive it back."

"I can get it in the morning," Monica offered. "Come on, let's get you into bed now."

When the two women went inside, Ethan gently set Trina down and kept a protective arm around her.

"It was a pretty bad episode this time," Carmen started, but her walkie-talkie crackled to life. "Tell Monica that I'll swing by in the morning and give her a lift to get her car."

Ethan waved her off and would've bundled his daughter into the safety of his truck and taken her straight home, but when he opened his passenger door for her, she shook her head. "Tootie's still in the house. I have to go get her."

Monica was just coming down the stairs when they got into the entryway. "Ethan, I am so sorry that this happened on my watch."

"Don't worry about it. Everyone is safe and sound. Besides, how could you have stopped it?"

"That's what's eating me up. I couldn't stop it, short of locking Gran up and turning our home into a prison."

"It's my fault," Trina said, her lips curled downward as

the toe of her sneaker tapped at a dark spot on the hardwood floor. "I just didn't want her to go alone. I called out to Monica, but I don't think she heard me over the record player. Gran kept calling me Bettina and saying, 'Don't tell Mom.'"

"Bettina is Gran's sister." Monica took off her glasses to rub the bridge of her nose. "Sometimes she has flashbacks to when she was a kid and gets the past confused with the present."

"Then I guess that would make you her mom?" Ethan suggested, not knowing what else to say. He didn't want Monica beating herself up over something she couldn't really control.

"Sometimes I feel like that." Her dark, silky hair was loose and curly and Ethan realized it was the first time he'd seen it out of a ponytail or messy bun. When was the last time she'd ever been able to actually let her hair down and relax?

"Well, I still shoulda ran and got you," Trina said, her face filled with remorse. "But she seemed so happy and I thought I could just…you know…take care of her myself. When we got to the ice cream place, though, she was all confused and didn't know who I was or who she was and I started to get real scared. The teenager behind the counter started yelling at her and Gran started yelling back and then the teenager called us nutjobs and threatened to call the cops if we didn't leave and that's when Officer Gregson showed up."

"*Mija*—" the older woman was holding her tap shoes in one hand as she came down the stairs "—I have a craving for some ice cream. Let's run into town and oh… Hi there, Ethan. What are you and Trina doing here?"

His daughter's eyes were wide and she took a step closer to him, but her courage surprised him when she spoke calmly to the older woman. "We already went to get ice cream, Gran. Remember?"

"Oh. That's right." Mrs. Alvarez turned to Ethan and it was as though he could see the entire events of the evening pass across her face as her memory returned. In fact, suddenly, the woman looked much older than her eighty-something years. "I hope you're not mad at me for getting arrested with your little girl."

"Nobody got arrested, Gran," Monica said, gently removing the dance shoes from the frail woman's bony hand. "Officer Gregson gave you a ride home because you seemed pretty confused."

"That's been happening a lot, huh, *mija*? Me getting confused."

Monica's eyes filled with tears, but she swiped them away quickly. Her voice broke when she replied, "Yes, Gran. You have Alzheimer's. It makes you forget things sometimes."

Mrs. Alvarez's face fell and Ethan could only imagine the complex emotions she was going through as the significance of the diagnosis settled over her. How many times had she and Monica probably had this same exact conversation, both of them reliving the painful revelation each time?

Nobody spoke for several seconds, until Gran reached out and stroked her granddaughter's upper arm. "I suppose it must be terribly difficult for you, taking care of me."

"You took care of me, Gran. It's only fair that I take care of you."

The older woman studied Ethan for several seconds before her eyes returned to Monica. "But when I took care of you, I'd already experienced the best years of my life. You're too young for such a burden, *mija*. You need to be out on dates and having fun and thinking about starting a family of your own."

"I already have a family, Gran." She lowered her voice before switching to Spanish. "*Tu es mi familia.*"

But the older woman shook her head as she patted Monica's hand. "Tell her, Ethan. Tell my girl that she should be going out on dates."

"I've been trying to get her out on a date for six months, Mrs. Alvarez." He shrugged, resorting to what came natural to him in tense, uncomfortable moments like these. Teasing. "But your granddaughter won't listen to me."

"If I was in a home, she'd go out with you."

"This *is* your home, Gran."

"Oh, *mija*, you know what I mean. I saw the brochure in the trash can last week. That one you brought home with the pictures of all those gray-haired people gardening and swimming in a big fancy pool and playing bingo. What was it called?"

"Legacy Village," Monica sighed, but her shoulders were ramrod straight and Ethan could tell that the fight hadn't left her. "It's a memory care center."

"Meh," her grandmother tsked. "They probably won't help me get my memory back, but maybe we should check it out all the same?"

"Gran, I'm not going to take you there."

"Then I'll have Ethan take me there. You'll take me right, *mijo*?"

"I'd rather take you out dancing, Mrs. Alvarez," he said, attempting another wisecrack to cover the fact that he wished he could be anywhere but there, thrust into the middle of an extremely personal family conversation.

"Oh, *mijo*, I'd spin circles around you. But Monica would love to go dancing with you."

"Gran," she warned her grandmother, and Ethan would've laughed at how tight Monica's jaw had locked down if his own wasn't still sore from clenching it a few minutes ago when he'd thought his daughter was missing again.

"There's a dance at the VFW for St. Patrick's Day," Mrs. Alvarez continued. "Why don't you two go to that?"

Monica said something about Gran's memory only working when it was convenient. Or inconvenient. He couldn't be sure because she'd mumbled the sarcastic remark under her breath.

"I'll tell you what, Mrs. Alvarez," Ethan replied. "Why don't we go over to Legacy Village on Saturday and check it out, then we can all go to the St. Patrick's Day dance afterward together?"

"Oh, what a brilliant plan. You're such a smart one." She patted his hand before looking at Monica. "Isn't he smart, *mija*?"

Monica narrowed her eyes as she sized up both of them. "I think the word you're looking for is sneaky."

On Saturday morning, Ethan and Trina arrived on Monica's front porch to take her and Gran to Legacy Village, just as he'd promised. Or threatened, depending on who was asked.

Monica had seen him on Tuesday and Thursday at the library, but they'd only talked about two things: how Trina's math tutoring was going—she was already learning tools for telling numbers and symbols apart. And how Gran was feeling—more episodes and forgetfulness this week, but so far no sneaking out of the house.

What Monica and Ethan still hadn't discussed was that heat-filled, mind-boggling and totally unexpected kiss a little over a week ago.

Maybe it hadn't made much of an impression on him, Monica decided after he still hadn't mentioned it when she'd ran into him and Trina getting sub sandwiches at Domino's Deli on Wednesday night. The man had probably kissed more women than he could count and her pathetic and awkward attempt at a make out session in the very public library was just another check mark for his man credentials.

So if Ethan could pretend that nothing physical had happened between them, then so could she. In fact, she was surprised that he'd shown up at all today.

"You guys made it," she said when she answered the door Saturday morning.

His wide shoulders went back and his chin went up. "Did you think we wouldn't?"

"I just know that most people wouldn't want to go tour a retirement home on their day off. I wouldn't have blamed you if you'd found something more fun to do. Like jumping a motorcycle across the Sugar River Gorge?"

Everyone in town knew that Ethan was quite the daredevil and adrenaline junkie. The other day in the library, Trina had mentioned the recent snowboarding and rock climbing excursions and how she needed to start downloading books onto her smartphone so she could read when he dragged her along on his adventures.

"Nope. Motorcycle jumping is always on Sundays." He wiggled his eyebrows before lowering his voice. "Besides, I would've blamed *myself* if I didn't make it today. Contrary to the way you always look down your nose at me, I don't take my promises or my commitments lightly."

Monica's throat grew tight. She wasn't ready to be one of Ethan's commitments. "I doubt Gran even remembers that you said you would come with us. Or, you know, about that other thing tonight."

Monica tried to give him a dismissive wave of her hand, hoping he'd forgotten about the second half of the bargain he'd made with her grandmother. But Ethan folded his arms across his chest. "It doesn't matter what Mrs. Alvarez remembers. If *I* say I'm going to do something, then I'm going to do it. Unless, of course, you found another date for the St. Patrick's Day Dance tonight?"

Oh great. He loudly mentioned the very thing she'd been trying to avoid right as Gran walked out of the kitchen with the handles of a wicker basket looped over her arm.

"That's right, the St. Patrick's Day Dance is tonight. I hope we're back from the picnic in time for you kids to go."

"Gran, we're not going on a picnic today." She shot Ethan a knowing look. *See, she wouldn't have remembered if you hadn't brought it up.* "We're going to Legacy Village to take a tour."

"Is that the old folks home?" her grandmother asked.

"It's a memory care center," Trina offered.

"Oh, and you brought Bettina with you."

"Actually, Gran that's not—"

"It's okay if she calls me that," Trina said softly, and Monica could've hugged the girl for being so understanding.

"Well, then what are we waiting for?" Gran asked as she walked out to Ethan's truck carrying the picnic basket. Her tap shoes pinged against the sidewalk, but at least she'd been willing to put on a pair of stretchy pants and a cardigan sweater over her favorite leotard instead of her old bathrobe.

"Thank you for always being so sweet with her," Monica whispered to Trina as they followed Ethan and Gran outside. "Sometimes, she mistakes me for her sister, too."

"Well, I've never been anyone's sister, so I don't mind."

"Me neither." Monica smiled and gave Trina's shoulder a little squeeze. The girl didn't flinch or back away, so they were definitely making progress.

Legacy Village was located near the military hospital, thirty minutes down the mountain. Monica sat quietly beside Trina in the back of the crew cab and tried not to look at the digital clock on Ethan's dash or think about how much time it would take to visit Gran every day. Or worse, to get to Gran if she had a major episode and needed Monica.

Her grandmother kept up a steady stream of conversation, regaling Ethan with tales of her glory days as a backup dancer in Hollywood during the sixties. "Have you seen my picture with Elvis?"

"The one on your fireplace mantel? I did see that," Ethan said for the fifth time in only ten minutes. "Did the King ask you for your autograph?"

Gran giggled and playfully swatted at Ethan's shoulder. "No, but he did ask me to teach him how to do the frug."

"What's the frug?" Trina asked.

"It's a dance where you…um…you move your… I can't exactly remember." Gran turned to look at Monica and her expression was slack, her eyes blinking several times. "How far away is this picnic, anyway?"

"We're almost there," Ethan said, and Gran's head snapped back to him. Alarm spread through Monica because her grandmother was now frowning.

"No. This isn't it. The Fourth of July picnic is always in Town Square Park and this is definitely not the way to Town Square Park." Gran's face had gone pale and she pivoted in her seat again, her eyes darting frantically between Trina and Monica as she clutched her purse against her chest. "Aren't you two going to stop him? The driver is taking us to the wrong place."

"Gran." Monica put a calming hand on the older woman's shoulder, but Gran jumped away from her, knocking her bony elbow into the dashboard. Monica's heart crumpled at the realization that her own grandmother was suddenly terrified of her.

"Stop calling me that. Where are you people taking me? I want to go back. Turn around. I'll call the police." Gran reached for the door handle, as if she planned to leap out of a vehicle doing fifty miles an hour down a two-lane highway. Thankfully, Ethan had locked the doors when they'd first gotten inside. He looked in the rearview mirror at Monica, his brows raised as though to ask her what she wanted him to do.

"Gran, it's me, Monica. Your granddaughter…" she started again, but her grandmother had managed to get her window halfway down and was yelling for help in Spanish. Luckily, the bike lane was empty, but what if someone thought they were abducting her? What if someone reported them to adult protective services? Fear paralyzed Monica as her brain ran through every worst-case scenario.

"Siri, play Elvis," Trina said into her smartphone and the beginning strains of "Viva Las Vegas" came out of the speaker. It took Gran a few seconds to recognize the intro of the congo drums, but by the time the King began crooning the chorus, Monica's grandmother was already breathing more steadily.

Monica's own breathing, though, didn't settle until the next song began and Gran started tapping her fingers along to the beat of "Suspicious Minds."

Exhaling through her nose, Monica slouched against the backseat, trying to get her heart rate under control. Suspicious minds, indeed. The appropriateness of the lyrics wasn't lost on her. Or on Ethan, apparently, who kept glancing at her in the rearview mirror.

"Hey, did I ever tell you guys that I have a photo of me with Elvis?" Gran asked, as though she hadn't been in full paranoia mode a few minutes ago, about to fling her frail body out of a moving vehicle in order to get away from the one person in the world who loved her the most.

"No kidding?" Ethan said casually, despite the fact that his fingers were still clenched around the steering wheel at the ten-and-two position. "I'd really love to see that picture sometime."

"It's on the fireplace mantel at home. Right next to Monica's college graduation picture. I always knew my *mija* would go to college."

"Did you ever go to college, Mrs. Alvarez?" Trina asked.

"I didn't even finish high school, dear. I had my first professional audition when I was fifteen. I had to lie about my age, of course…" Gran continued talking about her short-lived dance career and Monica closed her eyes as she massaged her temples, crisis temporarily averted. For now.

She'd read all the books, done all the research. She knew that people with Alzheimer's responded well to familiar music and stories about their youth. More important, she'd experienced Gran being confused and forgetting who she was at least several times a day. But her grandmother had never looked at her with those terrified eyes, as if Monica was out to hurt her or cause damage.

Instead of responding properly to the situation, though, Monica herself panicked and had just sat there frozen. Guilt washed over her as she replayed her own incompetence in bringing Gran down from such a chilling episode. Rather, it had been a quick thinking eleven-year-old who'd saved the day.

Chapter Ten

Monica knew within the first ten minutes of the tour that there was no way she could leave her grandmother at Legacy Village. It was too big, too full of people who also needed help—some appearing more incapacitated or dependent than her own grandmother. Gran could get lost in a place like this. Or worse, forgotten. But Monica smiled and nodded and followed the intake nurse, a middle-aged woman with purple hair and a name tag that said NICOLE in large print, as she showed them the independent living apartments and the water aerobics pool, and the full-service dining options.

"They sure have a lot of old people here," Gran said to no one in particular as they passed several residents parked in wheelchairs near the "Drive-In Theater," which was really just a big movie room with a huge screen on one wall and murals painted with old-fashioned cars on the other walls.

Monica didn't point out the fact that her grandmother was of a similar age as the majority of residents, and Trina kept her phone in her hand, probably prepared to play more Elvis songs in case another one of Gran's episodes began.

Nicole was talking to Gran about the activities calendar when Ethan put his hand on Monica's waist and leaned toward her. "So what do you think?"

"It's clean. And the people seem nice. But I don't think it's for Gran."

"She seems to like it so far." He nodded to Gran who was waving at a silver-haired woman hunched over a walker as though they were long-lost friends.

"Well, I'm sure they're only showing us the best parts."

"Now you sound like your neighbor Mr. Simon." Ethan didn't remove his hand and his lips lowered toward her temple. "He wrote down my license plate number the other day."

"He writes down everyone's license plate numbers. He also regularly posts to the neighborhood watch app every time Mrs. Fitzroy gets a package delivery because he thinks the UPS driver has the same style mustache as someone on the Crime Stoppers website."

"Exactly. Why do you guys always think the worst of people?" Ethan's warm breath against her hairline was currently preventing her from doing any thinking at all. Besides, Monica was only being cautious. She certainly wasn't as bad as Mr. Simon.

"Listen, I'm not saying there's anything wrong with the place. It's fine for other people's grandparents. But it's not what I want for Gran."

"It might not be what you want, but it's what she needs that matters."

"She *needs* to be home with me." Monica crossed her arms in front of herself, her determined stance causing Ethan to return to his full height. "Nobody here will love her the way I love her."

"Of course you love her. But are we just going to pretend that that incident in the car didn't just happen? She was terrified, Monica. Hell, *you* were terrified."

"Only because I was afraid of how it might affect Trina," she mumbled.

Ethan's sigh was heavy as he ran a hand through his hair. "Man, Trina was the only one of us who kept her cool. Even *I* reverted to my hostage extraction training and was about to jump across the bench seat and haul Gran against me to keep her from hurting herself."

"*Mija*, look, they have dance classes here." Gran pointed to something on the five-by-five-foot activity calendar on the wall. Geez, everything was written in such big letters around here. "It's called Music and Motion and it starts after dinner."

"Actually—" Nicole pushed a purple strand of hair behind her ear "—our usual dance teacher who leads that class just had hip surgery and we don't know when she'll be back."

"I could teach the class," Gran offered. Then she did a hop shuffle followed by a double brush-back in her tap shoes to prove it.

"You certainly could teach it," Nicole replied with a bright smile, as though she was perfectly accustomed to indulging irrational people in their false delusions. Monica immediately pegged the woman for a science fiction reader. "I bet the residents would adore having a sub for the usual teacher. But I should warn you, Mrs. Alvarez.

Many of your students aren't quite as mobile as you. Some might even need to stay in the chairs and just clap along."

Wait. What? They were actually going to let her grandmother teach a dance class? This could go wrong on so many levels.

"Um, I don't want to be a party pooper here or anything, but I'm supposed to go to a sleepover at Kayla Patrelli's house tonight," Trina said in a low voice meant just for her father. However, Monica was so on edge from the car ride there and the tour that was now taking way longer than she'd anticipated, that her senses were incredibly heightened, especially her hearing. "I've never been to one before and we're supposed to be at her family's restaurant at four o'clock 'cause her mom is gonna let us make our own pizzas."

"I can drive you back to Sugar Falls, Trina, and then return for Monica and Gran later." Ethan was being more than accommodating and Monica had to wonder if he was just trying to escape the crazy again. Was he worried that Gran would have a meltdown if they told her she couldn't go to the dance class?

"That'll never work, *mijo*," Gran told Ethan. "The St. Patrick's Day Dance starts at seven tonight and you promised you'd take my granddaughter. I can just stay here at the hotel after I teach my class. That way you two can go on your date and have the night to yourselves."

"Oh, Gran, no." Monica gulped and her cheeks burned in mortification. "I'm not going on a *date* with—" She stopped when she saw the confusion filling her grandmother's eyes. She didn't need a repeat of what happened an hour ago on the ride there. "I mean, it's not a hotel. It's a…." She looked at Nicole for some help.

"You know, oftentimes, we have potential residents

stay overnight. Sort of like a trial run. Mrs. Alvarez would be welcome to stay here tonight to try us out."

"Did you know that when I was living in Hollywood, a group of us girls auditioned to be dancers on a cruise ship?" Gran's eyes went bright and her smile was wide, making Monica hope this story would prove to be a happy distraction. "First-class meals included and we could travel the world while entertaining the guests and putting on shows. I was the only one who got a callback and my friend Darla was so jealous that I got hired and she didn't."

"I don't remember you ever mentioning working on a cruise ship, Gran," Monica said, used to these little detours and scrambling to navigate them back to the current issue at hand. Or in this case, avoid the current issue at hand, which was Monica going out with Ethan. Alone.

"Well, right before we set sail, I found out I was pregnant with your dad. I married your grandpa, and that was the end of that." Gran made a tsking sound and shook her head. "Aw, but you should have seen that ship, *mija*. It was so big and fancy. Kind of like this hotel."

Oh boy. The pleading look on the older woman's face clued Monica into the fact that this story wasn't just a diversion. Gran actually thought she would be reliving her youth. How could Monica deny her grandmother the opportunity?

Ethan must've sensed her train of thought because he leaned in again and said, "It's only one night."

After Ethan dropped Trina off at Patrelli's Italian Restaurant, he walked to his apartment to get ready for his first date with Monica.

Well, it wasn't exactly a date. At least, not the kind

Ethan had in mind when he'd first decided he'd wanted to ask Monica out all those months ago. On the way home from Legacy Village, she'd tried to tell him that they didn't need to go to the St. Patrick's Day Dance, but Trina had insisted that Gran would find out if they didn't go and would be very disappointed. Just like they'd all been disappointed to find out that the picnic basket Gran had packed contained only pickles.

What did one even wear to a St. Patrick's Day party, anyway? Besides green? The only thing he really knew about the holiday was that it involved corned beef and copious amounts of green beer. In fact, he'd always thought the celebrations were just an excuse to get drunk. And he definitely couldn't do that tonight. When Monica had suggested she meet him at the VFW hall, he'd made a joke about being the designated driver then told her he'd pick her up at seven.

Standing on her front step, Ethan's chest grew heavy with each knock. He refused to believe he was nervous because of her. He never used to get nervous around women. But the sight of Monica opening the door made him catch his breath. She was wearing a green, silky dress that hit just below her thighs. Her tan cowboy boots drew even more attention to her long, sexy legs.

She must've caught him staring, because she tugged at the ruffled hem of her dress. "Is it too short? Maybe I should go back inside and change."

"No, it's perfect. Sorry for staring, but I'm used to seeing you in jeans at the café and those long, skinny skirts you always have on at the library." He was also staring because he'd never seen a more incredible set of legs, but saying so out loud would certainly scare her off. "Is it new?"

Monica grabbed her purse and a denim jacket off the

table in the entryway. "No, I've had it since I was in high school. Apparently, I've grown a bit since then, but it was the only green item of clothing in my closet. You ready to get this over with?"

"Is going out dancing really going to be a chore for you?" he asked, trying not to sound insulted. It was definitely easier to come across as lighthearted and the life of the party when he had a few drinks in him.

"Sorry. It's not you. I'm just not into big crowds and parties and making small talk with everyone who'll be asking me about Gran."

Some people might ask her about Gran, but a few of the bolder ones would likely ask her about where she'd been hiding those legs. He held the truck door open for her. "So we'll make an appearance. Maybe dance to a song or two so we can honestly tell your grandmother that we participated. Then we'll take off and you can call and check on things at Legacy Village."

Monica ducked her head, but not before he caught the sheepish expression. "I've already called twice."

"Good. Now I don't feel so overprotective for already stopping by Patrelli's to make sure Trina had her phone charger in case she needs to get a hold of me."

"Oh my gosh, I can't even begin to thank Trina for all her help with Gran today, for being so patient and springing into action like that with the music. I owe that girl another trip to the mall."

"She'd probably rather have a trip to the bookstore. Or a new e-reader so she doesn't have to download everything onto her phone."

"Hmm." Monica gave a dreamy smile as she looked out the window. "I can't even believe she's the same girl that you brought into the café a few weeks ago. She's really bloomed since she's been with you, Ethan."

"You sound surprised."

She held up her palm. "I wasn't trying to offend you."

"No, I know. I'm surprised, too."

They parked and went inside the VFW. It was already crowded and he was holding Monica's hand again, but she was stiffer than usual. Man, he'd never had to work this hard to get a woman to relax around him. Was she embarrassed to be seen with him?

"It looks like an army of leprechauns threw up in here," Ethan said over the band doing their rendition of the Dropkick Murphys on stage. Big Rhonda and the Roadsters played most of the local gigs and always tailored their playlist for the occasion.

Monica wrapped her free arm across her waist, but at least she kept her head raised. "I heard the kids at the elementary school did the shamrocks and pots of gold decorations."

"That explains why there's so many rainbows made out of construction paper. I was beginning to question the crafting skills of my fellow veterans."

Her smile was tight, as though she appreciated his joke, but was too uncomfortable to actually laugh out loud. "The VFW is donating 25 percent of the proceeds back to the school tonight. So I guess we better do our part and grab something to drink."

This was it. Ethan steeled his courage and gave a nod as he followed her over to the crowded bar.

Seeing the rows of liquor bottles lined up against the mirrored shelves behind the bartender no longer made him sweat with the inner battle of denying himself something he desperately wanted. Nor was he threatened by the fact that the bartender was married to one of the guys in his Monday night meetings and would surely tell her husband that Ethan had relapsed if he ordered anything stronger than a soda. No, the thing that had him gritting his teeth and pushing up the long sleeves of his black shirt was the conversation that would be sure to follow after he ordered.

"I'll take a pint of Guinness," Monica said to the bartender over the deafening sound of the bagpipes the lead singer was attempting to play.

"I'll have a Diet Coke," Ethan finally said, and the woman behind the bar gave him a slight nod of approval. Not that they both weren't well aware that an alcoholic could easily get their hands on a drink at a party like this.

Monica tilted her head and, before she even opened her lips, Ethan knew what her question would be. "You're not having a beer? It's St. Patrick's Day."

Unless it was an old Navy buddy who didn't know he'd gotten sober, Ethan could usually respond with a simple explanation of *I don't drink* and those who were polite didn't push. But Monica deserved to know the full truth instead of a puzzling nonresponse.

"You know those meetings I go to on Monday nights?" he asked and watched her face as the pieces fell into place. "They're AA meetings. I'm an alcoholic, Monica."

She didn't flinch or back away in disgust and she didn't narrow her eyes at him. However, she did study him for an uncomfortable amount of time without saying anything.

The weight of her stare settled over him despite the fact that his head was pivoting around to everyone else in the hall so that he wouldn't have to make eye contact with her. Ethan's fingers began twitching and he scratched the back of his neck.

"I changed my mind," Monica told the bartender when

the woman set a frothy pint on the polished oak in front of them. "I'll have a Diet Coke, too."

"No," Ethan replied immediately, his skin prickling with unease. He gave the bartender a pointed look and said, "No, she'll keep the Guinness."

Monica put a hand on his bicep, but his muscles were far too tight for her touch to penetrate his senses. "Ethan, if you're not going to drink, then—"

"Don't do that, Mon. Don't treat me differently now that you know."

"I'm not trying to treat you differently. It's just that I don't want to..." She trailed off, the same way most people did when they didn't know how they should act in front of an alcoholic.

"Tempt me?" he asked, then tried to ease the awkwardness by giving her a wink. "Listen, that dress you have on is way more tempting than some bitter, dark draft beer."

His words had the desired effect and a warm blush spread across her cheeks. He watched the muscles in her neck constrict as she swallowed before replying. "Honestly, it's okay. I don't even drink that often. The only reason I ordered it was because everyone else had them and I thought it would help me relax."

"Well, I'm all for you relaxing—" he passed the beer to her "—and cutting loose a little bit."

It was then that her eyes narrowed. The last thing he wanted was for her to think he was going to try to take advantage of her. Or couldn't be trusted.

"Fine." He took the beer back and handed it to the bartender, who was now ignoring her other customers and actively watching their conversation. "She'll have a Diet Coke. But keep the Guinness on my tab and give it to one of those ol' boys at the end of the bar over there."

Monica followed his nod toward several older men who'd probably never been to Ireland but were wearing matching green sashes and tweed caps and singing along to "Whiskey in the Jar."

Ethan took their diet sodas and they made their way to an abandoned table in the corner, but not before several local townspeople said hello or tried to wave them over toward the dance floor. Ethan gave most people a nod, but Monica kept her eyes faced forward as though she didn't see anyone or anything except for the safety of the perimeter of the room.

Yep, the gossips' tongues would be wagging tonight. He pulled out a metal folding chair for Monica and then moved another one closer beside her so they could talk without having to yell over the music.

His date might be shy, but she was also intelligent and curious, so it didn't take her long to ask, "So how long have you been…uh…"

"Sober?"

She nodded as she took a sip from her straw.

"Almost eighteen months."

"Do you still struggle with it?"

"I'd be lying if I said I didn't. Every day can be a struggle, but some days are easier than others. And I've gotten much better at knowing my red flags and staying in tune with what my body needs."

"What do you mean 'what your body needs'?" she asked, and he couldn't stop himself from looking down at her bare legs, her thighs more exposed by the way her dress had shifted higher when she sat down. She followed his gaze and cleared her throat.

He didn't bother to hide his guilt behind his smirk. "When I'm excited or angry or full of energy, my body craves an outlet, a way to release some of the adrenaline I tend to build up. When I'm bored or lonely or thinking about things that I've messed up in the past, my body craves a distraction to keep me from dwelling on all the crap. I used to use alcohol to regulate both, but that's no longer an option. Part of the appeal when I made my decision to move to Sugar Falls was the fact that there's no shortage of extreme sports here to keep me engaged."

"I heard you were an adrenaline junkie."

"You could say that."

"Sounds like being a Navy SEAL was the perfect job for you."

"It was. Until it wasn't."

The lines above her nose creased into a V. "Why do I feel like there's a story behind that?"

He gave a light chuckle, but his chest felt hollow inside. "Let's save that story for our second date."

"Ethan." She turned her shoulders toward him and took a deep breath. "It's one thing to joke about this being a date, but I think we both know that nothing serious can happen between us."

"Do we *both* know that? Because I have a feeling *you* only came to that conclusion after you found out about me being in recovery."

"No, that has nothing to do with it." She leaned forward. "I'll admit that I toyed with the idea of going out with you, but that was before."

"Before you found out I was an alcoholic?" he asked and took a gulp of his soda, wishing it had just a splash of something stronger to sting his throat. To burn away the shame filling his chest.

"No. Before Trina showed up and Gran got worse and we both had to deal with all these other complications of having family members depending on us." She pushed her glasses up farther on her nose, the serious librarian about to call him to task. "My whole life is centered around my grandmother right now and it wouldn't be fair to get involved in a relationship when I can't fully commit to it. You can't honestly tell me that your life hasn't been thrown out of whack by finding out you have a daughter."

"It one hundred percent has been thrown off." He rolled his shoulders back as though he was preparing to do some heavy lifting. "But hell, I was never really relationship material to start with. Nobody is saying we need to commit to anything, Mon. But if you're attracted to me and I'm attracted to you, I don't see why we can't spend time together and help each other out with mutual needs."

One eyebrow shot above the rim of her glasses. "Mutual needs?"

Crap. He used to be much smoother at this sort of thing.

"Okay, that didn't come out the way I meant. I just know that I like being with you. I also like helping you out. Listen, we can both agree that we have too much going on to get serious about anything else, but we also both needed someone to step in and ease the tension. Come on, don't you ever need a break?" He hesitated. "A physical release?"

"Physical release?" she hissed, looking at the nearby tables, probably to make sure nobody overheard them. Her cheeks were now stained pink, her full lower lip twisted between her teeth as she watched him. "I hope this is your way of asking me to be your partner for one of your extreme sports."

"Right now, I just want you to be my dance partner," he said when the strains of "Danny Boy" started. He stood up and pulled her to her feet. "We can discuss how extreme and how physical we want to get after that."

Chapter Eleven

Monica let Ethan pull her close on the dance floor, her body fitting perfectly against his.

She'd known that there were AA meetings at the community rec center on Monday nights, but she hadn't even put two and two together and figured out that was where he went when he'd leave Trina at her house.

That's how blind she'd allowed herself to become when it came to the man.

Not that it should matter that he was a recovering alcoholic, but having experienced her own father's preferences for addiction over family and everything else, Monica couldn't help but think of Ethan differently now.

The problem was that her body didn't think of him differently. Her arms still had a will of their own as they wrapped around his neck and her hips took charge of everything else below as they swayed against him.

When the song ended, he didn't release his grip from her waist, but he did lean back and wait for her to lift her head from his shoulder. "So we've officially fulfilled our promise to your gran. Now what?"

Now we go home and never see each other again, was what she should've said. However, it wasn't like she could simply avoid him or go back to pretending that he was just some flirtatious customer she could forget about at the end of her shift. They would obviously have to interact in the future, their lives in this small town were already too intertwined.

His gaze was heated, his grin was smug and his earlier words were still ricocheting inside her head.

Don't you ever need a break? A physical release?

From the very center of her core nestled against him, to her fingertips resting along his open collar, Monica ached with a need for some sort of release. As he waited for her answer, the challenge hung in the air between them. If he'd just put the proverbial ball in her court, the least she could do was control what happened from here on out.

There were plenty of things in her life right now that she couldn't control, including her body's reaction to him. If they got the physical stuff out of the way once and for all, though, her mind would be able to focus on the bigger picture around her. And Ethan Renault was definitely not a part of Monica's bigger picture.

She'd already made it clear that neither one of them were in any position to enter into a serious relationship, and really, a carefree bachelor like him would be grateful that she didn't want anything more.

This was the type of relationship her mom had warned her about. The kind where she didn't use her head, and put her own physical needs first. Yet, if she was careful—and

Monica was always careful—she should be able to keep things strictly physical with Ethan. That way, her heart would stay safe and her mind would stay sane.

Monica might've wrestled with the decision all night, but a shimmying, eighty-something-year-old in a green leather bustier and shamrock-shaped sunglasses wiggled up beside them and tossed a plastic strand of beads over Ethan's head.

"Hey, Lieutenant Renault, you gonna stand here all night making schmoopie eyes at my favorite waitress or are you two gonna dance?" Freckles asked.

"That depends." Ethan lifted his dark brow at Monica.

"You only live once, darlin'." Freckles winked at her before stage-whispering, "I don't think I need to tell you what *I'd* do if I had a man like *him* looking at me like *that*."

Monica nearly shrieked out loud as her boss gave her a playful swat on the rear before boogying off. Swallowing down her embarrassment and not wanting to cause any more of a scene, Monica finally answered Ethan's original question about what to do next. "Now we go back to my place."

She didn't have to repeat herself. He was already holding her hand, pulling her through the crowd of people who'd arrived late. If they hadn't left their jackets and her purse at the table, she was sure Ethan would've hauled her straight to the car right then. As it was, it took them another five minutes to collect their things because people kept stopping them to ask about Gran.

By the time they got to the parking lot, Monica's cheeks were sore from the fake smile she'd pasted on every time she'd told a neighbor or an old friend that her grandmother was doing as well as could be expected.

Her nerves were shot and her pulse was humming from Ethan's steady grip and the way he'd stayed by her side, continuously steering her away from any uncomfortable conversations as he guided her toward the exit.

"Normally, I try to duck out of a party with nobody seeing me," she admitted when they got to his truck. "But that was the smoothest, quickest escape I've ever had to suffer through. How did you learn to work a room like that?"

"Hostage negotiation training."

Of course. He'd been a part of one of the most elite special forces in the military. Not that she planned to go up against him in battle, but it was a reminder that he was likely more skilled when it came to outmaneuvering and outstrategizing.

Ethan shifted into reverse and then put his arm across the seat. But instead of looking out the rear window, he lifted his fingers and toyed with one of her loose curls. "So, we're going back to your place?"

"Yes," she said, then gulped, hoping he didn't hear the quiver in her voice. "But we should establish a few guidelines."

"What kind of guidelines?"

"The usual, I guess. You probably have more experience in this department than me."

"Are we talking about sex?"

"*Casual* sex," she clarified.

"Right. And you think *I'm* more experienced?"

"Than me? Definitely."

"Sounds like you don't know me very well."

"Okay, then let's start there." She hadn't gone through the same training as him, but she'd once read a book about negotiations. Hopefully, that was close enough to at least give off the appearance that she knew what she was talking about. "Rule one. No need to get to know each other that well. This is just physical. It's not a job interview."

"We're going to have rules?" Ethan's fingers tapped against the seat back. "Sounds pretty job-like if you ask me."

"Rule two," she continued. "Our families and our work come first. So we can only…you know…be together when we're not otherwise occupied."

"Rule three," he countered. "Let's not have so many rules."

"No, we need them to keep us from taking this attraction to the next level. It would be good for both of us if we set out the boundaries ahead of time."

His heat-filled gaze across the dim lights of the dashboard was just as intense as a caress, causing a shiver to race down her spine. "I will never do anything that would make you uncomfortable, Mon. At least, not on purpose. Contrary to what you might think about me, I'm not totally undisciplined. I do have some self-control."

"I don't think you're undisciplined," she protested.

He chuckled. "Are you trying to convince me? Or convince yourself?"

"I'm convinced that you're the only regular customer in the café who always orders the same healthy breakfast every morning. A boring diet like that takes a lot of discipline."

"Hmm," he replied, not sounding completely persuaded by her weak example as he finally backed out of the parking lot.

Okay, so maybe Monica *had* doubted his self-control, especially when it came to him being around so many alcoholic drinks at the VFW earlier. She'd read that addicts often lied to cover up their vices. In fact, Ethan's unsuitability worked in her favor because it would allow her to get close to him physically, while requiring her to maintain her distance emotionally.

He remained quiet throughout the short drive to her house and didn't say anything as he followed behind her up to the front porch, waiting patiently while she unlocked the door and then switched on the light in the entryway. It was odd enough going inside and not having Gran there waiting for her, but Ethan's silent and controlled movements were even more unsettling. Either he was holding himself back, waiting for her to change her mind. Or he was conserving his energy, a predator preparing to pounce upon his prey.

Sliding the dead bolt home gave her a boost of courage, a feeling of being the one in command. The decision had been made and Ethan was still here, watching her as she stood there shifting her weight from one leg to the other. "So how does this work? Do I offer you some coffee or something, or do we just head straight upstairs?"

"You mean you haven't already put a rule in place for one-night stands?"

The phrase made her wince, even though Monica had been the one to originally introduce the option of casual sex. "Is that what this is? A one-and-done kind of thing?"

"Rule four," he said, closing the distance between them. "Let's not put any time limits on anything."

Cupping her cheek, his face was only inches away from hers. He lifted his other hand and gently removed her glasses and set them on the small entry table. She could feel the ruffle along the V-neckline of her dress flutter against her chest as it rose and fell. One deep breath. Two deep breaths. Three… When his lips melded against hers, she didn't think about any more breaths or any more rules. She didn't think about anything but being closer to him and the barrier of his shirt that was now the only thing standing in her way.

Her fingers worked frantically over the buttons while her tongue dove in deeper in an attempt to stake her claim inside his mouth. When she finally got underneath, the heat from his bare chest set her palms on fire as she stroked every muscle, every ridge as though she needed to memorize the feel of him.

Something tugged against her arms and she moaned as her hands were pulled away from exploring his torso. But then she realized he was only relieving her of her jacket and her fingers returned to him as soon as she was free of the faded denim. His own hands slid to her hips and then behind to her rear end as he pulled her to him, pressing her against the hard length of desire under his zipper.

The house had grown chilly from the March evening and cool air kissed at the backs of her thighs as he slowly moved the silky fabric of her dress higher until it was bunched around her waist. Monica reached behind her to unzip the back, but his hands followed and one palm cupped the nape of her neck as he worked the zipper down.

His fingers trailed against her shoulders and she felt the dress delicately glide against her, bringing a heightened awareness to her skin as it dropped to the ground at her feet. Her bra followed the same route and the next thing she knew, she was standing in front of the man in nothing but her panties and her cowboy boots.

"Wow," he said, his voice low and throaty and warming every inch of her exposed flesh. When Ethan stared at her like that, Monica no longer felt shy or awkward.

She felt bold and powerful and capable of bringing a man to his knees. "I've spent the last six months imagining what you would look like when I finally got you naked, but nothing in my fantasies could've prepared me for how perfect the reality is. You are so much more than I expected."

"Finally got me naked?" she asked, reaching for his belt buckle. "You were pretty sure of yourself, huh?"

He lifted only one finger and traced it so lightly against her hardened nipple, her head tilted back as she whimpered.

"The only thing I was sure of was that I wasn't going to stop wanting you until I had you, Mon. And even now, I doubt that one time will be enough."

"Good, because I don't want to wait anymore." She brought her mouth back to his and kissed him deeply as she pressed her flat palms against the warm skin under his waistband, working his pants over the well-rounded curve of his butt until they joined her dress on the floor.

Ethan's hands were stroking and massaging and driving her mad as he hauled her against him. Breaking his lips away, he kissed a trail across her jaw, down her neck and to the same breast he'd been teasing earlier. He dropped to his knees in front of her, his hands continuing their descent over her hips, her thighs, her knees and her calves.

His lips had moved to the sensitive spot right below her belly button and after that, she didn't know where his hands went. Or what he'd done with her panties. Monica's breathing was already labored, but when Ethan's tongue dove into the center of her heat, she began to suck in quick gasps of air through her moans.

The first time she'd kissed him had been in the middle

of the book stacks at the library where anyone could've seen them. Now she was standing in the entryway of her house—still wearing her boots—as Ethan's tongue flicked and stroked and brought her to the highest peaks of desire. Apparently, her shameless response to him knew no bounds, and she no longer cared.

"I need you." Spreading her fingers through the short hair on his scalp, she eased his head up, watched him rise to his feet as his lips made their way back up to her face. "Now."

"You have me," he smirked. He walked her backward and when they got to the staircase, Monica thought he was going to lift her up and carry her upstairs.

But she didn't want to wait another second. She lowered herself to the second step, pulling him down with her. His lean hips slid between her thighs and she felt the rigid length of his manhood against the area he'd just so thoroughly kissed.

His chest pressed into her breasts and his face hovered over hers, his breath just as quick and frantic as hers when he asked, "Right here? On the stairs?"

She answered by pulling his lower lip into her mouth and suckling it.

His groan was low and a thrill shot through her at the knowledge that she could drive him just as wild as he was driving her.

"I need to grab something," he mumbled, but didn't take his eyes off her as he stretched an arm behind him and fumbled with his discarded pants. When he returned, he was already tearing open the package. As he rolled the condom on, the latex scent of the prophylactic mingled with the scent of her desire and Monica's thighs instinctively drew him closer, knowing her release was only moments away.

Pausing as his tip entered her, he closed his eyes and held himself perfectly still, as though he wanted to savor the moment. Monica drew in a ragged breath. "Ethan, please..."

With another groan, Ethan thrust forward, filling her as he lifted her hips. He wrapped his forearms against her waist, shielding her lower back from the wood planks of the stairs as he withdrew and plunged into her again and again. As the tempo built, Monica brought her knees around him, clinging tightly to every inch of him as her body shuddered and then shattered against him.

Ethan had never yelled out during sex before, but his ears were still echoing and his throat was hoarse from the way Monica's name had been torn from his mouth when he'd completely lost himself inside of her.

He eased his arms from behind her back and rested on his knees, which had never left the ground floor. Ethan couldn't believe he'd taken her right there on the stairs, but he certainly didn't mind the sight of her wearing nothing but a sheen of sweat and her cowboy boots.

His lips curved into a self-congratulatory grin as he stood and reached to pull her to her feet. She gave a contented sigh and his chest puffed out at the knowledge that he'd done a thorough job of satisfying her. So much for her one-and-done concern.

"Should we head to your room for round two?" he asked as he nuzzled his mouth against the warmth of her neck.

"I don't know if my legs are strong enough to climb the stairs yet."

"I've carried rucksacks heavier than you," he said before lifting her up vertically.

She let out a shriek before wrapping her calves around him again. He'd already made it up the first two steps when a muted ringtone sounded from his pants pocket on the floor below.

Monica stiffened before looking around frantically, probably to make sure they hadn't been caught again. Setting her back on her feet, he said, "Let me just make sure it's nothing important."

It took him a moment to dig the phone out of the pocket of his tangled pants. When he saw Trina's name on the screen, his heart jumped into his throat. "Hello?"

"Uh, hi. It's me. Trina." Her voice was hesitant and came out as a whisper, sending his pulse into overdrive. Something was wrong.

"What's wrong?"

"Oh, um, nothing?" There was a slight echo to her words and he told himself that she wasn't in any immediate danger.

"Are you in the bathroom?"

"Yeah? Um… I just wanted to see what you were doing?" Everything she said came out as a question.

Monica had already found her glasses and was pulling on her dress, concern etched all over her face. Obviously, he wasn't about to tell his daughter *exactly* what he was doing, but Trina knew he was supposed to be at a dance with Monica and she was smart enough to pick up on the fact there was no music playing in the background. "I was just dropping Mon off at her house. How are things going at the Patrellis'?"

Please say everything's okay, he thought. Not just because he wanted his daughter to be making friends and having a good time, but also because he wanted to continue having his own good time, as well. Man, that made him sound like a selfish ass.

"Um, it's okay, I guess? They have a lot of kids."

Ethan remembered spending the night at his best friend's house when he'd been the same age. The Phillips family also had a lot of kids and their house was full of noise and fun and arguments and life. He'd loved going over there and pretending he was just one more sibling. However, Trina wasn't the same way. She liked reading and listening to music by herself and anything else that involved being quiet. Which meant she was probably miserable over there.

Looking at Monica, her lips swollen and her cheeks raw from the whisker burn of his five o'clock shadow, Ethan swallowed a lump of disappointment and asked his daughter, "Want me to come pick you up?"

"No. Maybe. I don't want Kayla to think I'm a baby."

The fact that she was even admitting that much made Ethan want to run to her rescue.

"Why don't you tell her that Tootie won't settle down and go to sleep because she's missing you?" he offered. It was a valid enough excuse since that kitten had meowed like crazy at him after he'd returned to the apartment earlier this afternoon without Trina. "I'm leaving the Alvarez house now and should be there in about five."

He heard a sigh of relief coming from the other end. "Thank you, Dad."

The air left his lungs as he stared at the disconnected phone in his hands. It was the first time his daughter had actually called him Dad and not just in reference. A warmth spread through him and it felt as though the leader of the free world had just placed a medal of honor around his neck.

"Is everything okay?" Monica asked.

"Trina called me Dad," he said as he grinned stupidly at Monica. "She's never called me that before."

Monica's own mouth formed a surprise O before returning his smile. "That's incredible." Then her face dropped as she lifted her brows. "But did something happen at the Patrellis'?"

Ethan had done the casual thing with women before, but in his experience, a woman didn't appreciate being ditched before the night ended—no matter which call of duty summoned him. Monica had said she wanted to keep things physical and he was now about to put her wishes to the test.

"She didn't want to admit it, but she was a little nervous and would be more comfortable if I pick her up." He waited for a pout or an attempt to convince him otherwise.

"Poor Trina," Monica tsked before handing him his shirt. "I used to hate sleepovers when I was a girl. All that forced talking and staying up late and pretending to like another parents' cooking? It would always throw me off my routine and make me feel unsettled."

The way she shoved his shoes at him while he was still yanking a leg through his pants was beginning to make Ethan feel a bit unsettled himself. Apparently, she was pretty eager to see him leave. He tried not to be bothered by it. "So you don't mind if I take a rain check on coming upstairs with you?"

"Ethan, no promises or commitments, remember?" Her eyes darted around to everything else in the room but him as she reached behind her back to work up the zipper of her dress.

Unsure of whether her words were meant as a reminder that he didn't owe her anything, or a reminder that she wasn't guaranteeing anything in the future, he brought his finger to her chin and tilted up her face until she was forced to look directly at him. "You don't have to commit to anything, Mon. But I have no problem promising that I'm going to want you again. And soon."

Chapter Twelve

Monica pressed her fingers to her swollen lips after Ethan gave her a parting kiss.

Turning to climb the stairs, she avoided looking at the lower steps where they'd just made love. No, not made love, she corrected herself. They'd just had uncomplicated sex. Uncomplicated, mind-blowing, soul-reaching, earth-shattering sex.

And he'd promised to make her feel that way all over again. Perhaps they might even make it to an actual bed next time.

Nope, she wasn't going to go there, Monica told herself as she stepped into the hot shower and scrubbed the scent of his musky cologne off her skin. She shouldn't be looking forward to there even being a next time. Monica would never depend on a man for anything, not even uncomplicated, mind-blowing, soul-reaching, earth-shattering sex.

Especially from a man that had a history of leaving

town when a better offer came along. While Ethan might currently be proving himself to be a decent father, Monica knew that it couldn't last forever. Even a supposedly reformed bad boy might eventually get restless and take off. Although, he hadn't hesitated to go get Trina when she'd called and wanted to come home. In fact, he'd been downright giddy at the fact that his daughter had finally called him Dad. So at least the man's priorities were in order. For now.

When she climbed into her bed, her head barely hit the pillow before she was fast asleep. She slept hard and deep and didn't so much as dream until something startled her awake and she shot up in her bed. The house was way too dark and way too quiet.

Gran.

She'd forgotten to check on her. Monica's bare feet padded quickly down the dark hall toward her grandmother's room and when she saw the quilt perfectly made up on the bed, a kernel of panic rose in her chest. The digital clock with the jumbo numbers beside Gran's bed blinked 3:06 a.m. And then her sleepy brain finally clicked into place and she remembered her grandmother was staying at Legacy Village tonight.

See. Getting involved with Ethan was already making Monica forget about her responsibilities. Bringing him home last night had been a huge mistake.

Monica raced downstairs and held her breath as she fumbled in her purse, looking for her cell phone and praying she wouldn't find any missed calls from her grandmother. She let out a deep exhale when the screen came up blank. Nicole, the intake nurse, had told her that she could call the nursing desk anytime to check on Gran. But surely they would've notified her by now if there had been any problems. Carrying her phone back to her bed, Monica vowed to put all thoughts of Ethan out of her mind and to try to go back to sleep.

Unfortunately, she tossed and turned the rest of the night, reliving every touch, every kiss and every stroke.

Monica drove straight to Legacy Village on Sunday morning, finding a happy Gran holding court at the breakfast buffet and showing a woman wearing zebra-print slippers and a plastic tiara how to use the waffle iron.

"Look, Hector—" Gran reached across the toppings station and passed the can of whipped cream to an elderly man with the biggest earlobes Monica had ever seen "—my granddaughter's plane finally landed. How was the flight, *mija*?"

"My name is Gary, lady," the man grumbled before putting the whipped cream and three bananas into the hidden compartment under the seat of his walker and shuffling off.

"Are you ready to go home, Gran?" Monica asked, casting another look at Gary, who grabbed a few spoons out of the silverware caddy and slipped them into his pocket.

"Already?" her grandmother asked. "Can't we stay another night at the hotel? Please?"

Monica observed all of the residents sitting at their little tables in groups of four and six. The dining room was decorated more like an upscale country club than the Cowgirl Up Café, but it was just as crowded and lively as the Sugar Falls restaurant on a Sunday morning.

"But we always make *sopa* together on Sunday nights." Really, just like the enchiladas, Gran made everything herself while Monica just supervised.

"*Mija,* you know how to make *sopa* just fine by your-self. Besides, they're having church services at ten. They have a lady minister who comes in and we don't even have to go anywhere. Then they're having a piano player this afternoon and obviously they're going to need someone to lead the dancing." Gran lowered her voice to a whisper, "Some of these people are so stiff and bored, they don't even get up to dance unless someone encourages them."

Probably because more than half of the residents ap-peared to have limited mobility, Monica thought as the wire basket on an electric scooter clipped her elbow, its occupant speeding by toward the omelet station.

"Good morning, Mrs. Alvarez." Nicole appeared, her hair in a sleek purple bob today. "I heard you had quite the active night last evening."

Monica's stomach sank as she braced herself for the worst. No telling what kind of mischief her grandmother had gotten into. Please don't let it involve fire damage or monetary compensation, Monica prayed silently. There was no way they could afford any more setbacks.

"So does that mean I'm gonna get the job?" Gran clapped her hands together.

"I think we can work out a suitable offer," Nicole re-plied. "Do you mind if I speak with your agent about it?"

Oh boy. Were they really going to keep up the cruise ship dancer pretense?

"Be straight with me," Monica told Nicole when Gran went to assist a resident who was falling asleep in his chair and losing his grip on his cream cheese-slathered bagel. "How did she do?"

"She was quite the spitfire," Nicole chuckled.

"I'm so sorry. I can take her home right now—"

"Monica, no." The nurse waved her palm back and

forth. "I didn't mean that in a bad way. I meant she was actually very energetic and helped liven things up around here. She even got a conga line going at one point. Then last night's movie was *Blue Hawaii*, so she was practically a celebrity. The night nurse said she slept soundly until six this morning and then found her way to the kitchen and helped Reynaldo get the bacon and sausage going for breakfast."

"Oh no, you can't let Gran near a stove without proper supervision."

"Monica." Nicole folded her hands together in front of her chest. "I understand that you know your grandmother better than we do. But we want our residents to engage in the normal activities they're used to doing at home. Everyone on our staff—from our electrician to our chef to our night janitors—is trained to supervise and engage with residents just like Mrs. Alvarez. We have locks and security measures in place where we need them, but we also have a wealth of compassion and understanding for what our residents are missing from their old lives."

Monica sighed. "I just don't want her to get hurt. Or endanger others."

"I'm not going to promise that she won't ever have mishaps. Her condition is going to get worse and she's going to start having more bad days than good. We understand that she can't help it and we certainly don't expect perfect behavior from any of our residents. But we're well equipped to deal with any situation that comes up."

It was more than Monica could say for herself.

"Why don't you bring down some of her things and let her stay for the entire week and see how she does before you make a decision?" Nicole suggested. "No promises or commitments."

No promises or commitments. Monica's heart sank at the phrase that was now becoming all too familiar in her life.

On Sunday evening, Ethan went back and forth with whether he should call Monica. Mostly, he just wanted to hear her voice and know that she wasn't mad at him for leaving so abruptly on Saturday night. But he also was curious to find out how her grandmother had done with the sleepover at Legacy Village.

He paced along the boxes stacked against his bedroom wall until Tootie began attacking his foot every time he did an about-face, swatting at the shoelace on his hiking boot. In the past couple of weeks, her tiny kitten teeth had chewed through the laces of one of his favorite pairs of running shoes and both of his work boots. She'd also shredded through several toilet paper rolls; regularly used the ugly orange sofa as a scratching post; and tore up the school cafeteria menu he'd taped to the refrigerator, as well as the math worksheet Trina had "accidentally" forgotten on the kitchen table.

They'd learned to close the bathroom door before leaving the house, as well as put all their shoes away in the closets. But the poor sofa was out of luck until Ethan had time to build a mini cat condo. Trina said that Tootie was punishing them for abandoning her during the day to go to school and work. But the thing was a cat. Wasn't she supposed to want to be left alone?

Alone. Tomorrow was his Monday night meeting and he still needed someone to watch Trina for him. Ethan's mind sprang into action. That would be a perfect excuse to call Monica.

Unfortunately, his daughter was reading a book in the living room and, with the thin walls of his apartment, he didn't want her overhearing anything in the event Monica said she couldn't watch her. Trina didn't need any added rejection in her life.

Ethan pulled his phone out of his pocket as the first pricks of Tootie's claws began their assent up the leg of his jeans. He scooped her up and put her on his shoulder, which, other than Trina's lap, was the kitten's favorite place to be. Unfortunately, he got rewarded for his efforts with a puff of gas from under her tail.

"Geez, cat, what did you eat?" He scrunched up his nose as he started a text to Monica. How did your gran do with her trial stay at the place?

The little bubble popped up on his screen, indicating that she was responding and Ethan shuddered. Although, the sensation probably came from Tootie's whiskers as she used her nose to explore the area behind his ear.

Gran did really well. In fact she wanted to stay longer, surprisingly. Nicole said she could extend the trial to a week so I drove home and packed some of Gran's things and her blood pressure meds, then went back to have dinner with her and sign some papers. I just got home and I'm drained.

Did you get any sleep? he began to type then quickly deleted the words. It would've been a good opening to bring up what they'd done last night, however, he didn't want to scare her off too quickly. Are you working to-morrow?

Yes. Both jobs. Then I was thinking that Trina and I could go down and visit Gran while you're at your meeting.

Thank God she'd brought it up so he didn't have to sound like a jerk for wanting to add more responsibility to her already full plate. Are you sure you don't mind having Trina tomorrow? I know things have changed with your gran and I don't want to inconvenience you.

Trina's not an inconvenience. And Gran will want to see her. The response bubble popped up again and then disappeared, as though she too had just deleted something.

Were you going to add that YOU wanted to see ME, as well?

Actually, I was going to add that I didn't want you to miss your meeting.

"She thinks I lack self-control," he explained to Tootie, who'd curled herself into a ball on his shoulder.

And maybe he did, because he couldn't stop himself from typing, Well, I'm looking forward to seeing you. Maybe after my meeting we can pick up where we left off?

Bubbles appeared then disappeared at least three times and Ethan chuckled at how flustered she must be if she kept deleting her responses. Finally she replied, Not in front of your daughter.

His mouth lifted at the corners. She hadn't completely shot him down. She was merely forcing him to make some adjustments to his launch coordinates.

Luckily, Ethan didn't try anything in front of his daughter when he'd dropped her off earlier Monday evening. Probably because Monica planned ahead and already had her purse and keys in her hand when they'd pulled up to her house.

Tootie was a hit with the residents at Legacy Village—especially with Hector/Gary, who'd tried to sneak the kitten into the hidden compartment of his walker and take her back to his room with the rest of the items he'd pocketed along the way.

Her grandmother had been happy to see her and Trina at first, but then Gran had switched into her cruise director mode during bingo, ditching them to stand in front of the room and calling out the numbers. When they'd left, Gran had acted as though she didn't even know them and said, "Have a safe flight home."

Monica was exhausted and slightly depressed when she and Trina got into the car to return to Sugar Falls. On the return trip, they talked about her upcoming book report for school and Tootie's new diet and maybe trying to stay over at Kayla Patrelli's house again. But Monica knew something else was still on the girl's mind as they drove home, because she didn't even bother with her headphones.

The one subject Trina hadn't brought up so far tonight was her father. As much as Monica didn't want to discuss the man either, she had a feeling that Ethan was the looming elephant in the room—or the car, so to speak. If she didn't steer the conversation in that direction, how would she know if Trina was truly doing okay?

"So, how do you like living in Sugar Falls?" Monica asked, chickening out at the last moment.

"I like it." Her reply was simple and followed by silence. So apparently, that subject was a dead end.

"How about your apartment? Are you and Tootie pretty comfortable living there?"

"It's okay. It kinda smells like pastrami all the time because we live on top of a deli. My dad said the caseworker is going to come Wednesday afternoon and check us out. I kinda..." Trina's voice trailed off.

"You kinda what?" Monica pushed.

"I kinda wish it had more decorations in it, like your house does. I don't want the caseworker to think it's too plain, like it could belong to anyone."

"You mean you want it to look lived-in?"

The girl kept her head down as she stroked Tootie's gray fur. "Yeah. I want her to think it's a good place for me to stay."

Monica's heart stretched and her throat tightened. Trina *wanted* to stay with her father. Ethan would be so happy to know this. "If you want, I can bring some stuff over tomorrow to help spruce the place up."

Trina's face lifted, revealing a bright smile. "Maybe some stuff from your house? I don't want to get anything brand-new because then it will look obvious, like we're trying too hard. And pictures. We'll need some pictures in frames."

The kid was smart, Monica had to give it to her. "I definitely have some old frames. But we'll have our work cut out for us if we need to decorate *and* get some photos made up in less than forty-eight hours."

"I've been taking a few on my phone, but maybe we should get a shot of all of us together."

"All of *who* together?" Monica asked, her knuckles stiffening as she gripped the steering wheel.

"You, me, Dad and Gran."

Oh no. The poor child was under the impression that they were some sort of family unit, or at least she was hoping to portray them as such. A nugget of shame lodged in Monica's belly and she knew the thing would only get bigger if she didn't level with Trina.

"I don't know if…" Monica started, but didn't know how to finish without insulting the girl or making her feel rejected.

"I don't mean like a family photo or anything. But just something showing that me and Dad have what they call 'a support system.'" Trina was smart *and* she'd done her research.

Monica slowly exhaled. "If it's okay with your dad, then it's okay with me."

"Are you kidding? My dad will do anything if you tell him to. I know he asks your advice for stuff all the time. And he's always staring at you with those googly eyes."

"Your dad does not have googly eyes," Monica replied, already regretting the curiosity lacing her voice. Really, Ethan's eyes always were sort of empty and hard to read, even when he'd been flirting with her at the café. At least they used to be. Before Trina had arrived. Now they were mostly full of confusion and concern and occasionally lust.

"I know you guys kissed." Trina was now staring directly at her. Monica kept her eyes on the road, but the girl's scrutiny continued to drill into her.

Shifting in her seat, she asked, "How do you know he kissed me on Saturday night?"

"I was talking about when I saw you in the library, remember? Why? Did you kiss *again* after your date?"

Monica's brain spun as excuses pinged through her mind. She wanted to deny everything, but Trina was too old and too smart not to see through it. Pulling up to the first stoplight in town, Monica decided she'd have to change tactics. "Honey, I want you to know that *you* are your father's main priority. No matter what happens between him and me, we will always think about you first. Both of us only want to do what's best for you."

"So then you *are* dating?" Trina's lids lowered the same way they did when she was calculating math problems with her tutor in the library, but she didn't so much as blink. "Like officially?"

"No, not officially. We're just friends," Monica said as she turned onto her street. Ethan's truck was already waiting at the curb in front of her house. "I think."

Chapter Thirteen

"Hi, Dad," Trina said when she opened the door. The kitten, startled awake by the dome light, suddenly jumped out and made a beeline for the bushes. "Tootie! Come back!"

Just when Monica didn't think her nerves could handle any more stimulation tonight, Ethan took off after the animal.

"I'll get her," Ethan said, getting flat on his belly under the thick hedge of junipers along the property line. He made several mewing sounds before pleading with the kitten, "Come here, Tootie, that's a good girl. You want a little piece of cheese? Daddy will get you a little piece of cheese if you come out…"

"What in the heck are you doing?" Mr. Simon muttered from the other side of the hedge, making Tootie scamper deeper into the dense branches.

"I'm trying to get my daughter's kitten out of the

bushes." Ethan stood up and brushed the dirt off his chest and flat abdomen before looking over the five-foot-tall hedge at her neighbor. "Why are you wearing night vision goggles?"

"I heard some kids were gonna be out toilet papering tonight and I plan to catch them in the act." Mr. Simon was dressed in all black and his camouflage face paint only made the grooves of his wrinkles stand out. "But if they see you all out here having a party, they'll likely get scared and take off."

"You know you can call the police to handle that sort of thing," Ethan offered.

"Already did. But Officer Gregson says they don't have the resources to conduct an all-night stakeout, so here I am."

A rustling sounded in the branches and Ethan dropped back down to the ground. "Come on, Tootie," he pleaded again. But the cat didn't seem to care.

"I thought you were supposed to be a Navy SEAL." Mr. Simon shifted his night vision goggles to rest on top of his receding hairline. "What kind of Navy SEAL can't get a little cat out of some bushes?"

"Monica." Ethan twisted his neck to glance up at her. Even from that angle and in the dim glow of the street-light, she could tell that he was having a tough time keeping his grin in check. "Could you please get me a slice of cheese so I can bribe the cat out without having to resort to my elite spec ops skills to navigate through this maze of juniper branches? Preferably before Mr. Simon asks to see my DD214 forms as proof of my service."

"Aye, aye, Lieutenant." Monica gave a mock salute before heading inside to the kitchen. When she returned,

Trina was on her knees beside her dad making clicking sounds and calling for her kitten.

The girl turned to Monica. "Mr. Simon was just telling us that he read a book about a cat burglar who literally stole people's cats."

"Yep. The Feline Felon. You know, they never did catch him." Monica's retired neighbor really needed to find a new hobby. Considering the size of this overgrown hedge separating their yards, maybe Monica should refer him to the gardening section the next time he came to the library.

"Hurry, Dad," Trina said, using her phone's flashlight app as Ethan took the wrapped slice Monica had just handed him.

Monica glared at Mr. Simon before kneeling on the ground to get a better look. "Nobody's going to steal Tootie."

Ethan didn't even need to hold the cheese out. The kitten was already sashaying out of the branches at the sound of the cellophane wrapper.

Trina scooped Tootie up quickly and chastised her while simultaneously nuzzling the gray fur on the animal's neck.

"We better get this little escape artist home." Ethan handed his daughter the yellow cheese before standing up. After he'd brushed himself off again a second time, he scratched the cat behind her ears as Trina fed her. The trembling sensation in Monica's lower regions was no doubt coming from her ovaries.

Walking toward his truck, Ethan asked Monica, "How was Gran?"

"She was okay. Didn't know who we were after the first thirty minutes, but she seemed really happy to be at that place. Don't you think, Trina?" Monica apparently now needed the confirmation of an eleven-year-old girl to justify that it was okay to put her grandmother in a home.

"She sure was smiling and laughing a whole lot," Trina replied, as she climbed into the front seat with Tootie cradled under one arm. "Hey, Dad, Monica said she's going to bring some stuff over to our house tomorrow so we can decorate for the home visit."

If Ethan didn't want Monica's involvement in his personal family business, now would've been the perfect time for him to speak up. Instead, he just smiled and dropped a kiss to Monica's temple. "Cool. We'll see you tomorrow, then. I'll make dinner for us."

Monica's face burned all the way to the roots of her hair.

"Can I tell the caseworker you guys are dating?" Trina asked her dad through the open window before looking at Monica. "I mean, you said you wanted to do the best thing for me and I think the best thing would be for the caseworker to know that my dad has a girlfriend and that she's part of our support system."

"What caseworker?" The question came from behind the bushes. "Like an investigator? What are they investigating?"

"Good luck with your stakeout, Mr. Simon." Ethan waved at the neighbor. "Let me know if you ever need to borrow my night vision goggles. They're modified with four tubes for a field of view of 97 degrees. They're also military grade and come complete with a government restriction."

A thumbs-up popped above the hedge and Monica squeezed her eyes shut behind her glasses to keep from rolling them.

When she opened her lids, Ethan was less than a foot away and her legs gave a wobble as she waited for him to kiss her, right there in front of his daughter. Again.

Instead of using his lips, though, the challenge in his eyes had a deeper impact on her nerves. "Bye, Mon. See you tomorrow at six."

Tuesday night, Monica arrived at the apartment carrying two boxes filled with quilts, throw pillows and some knickknacks that put Ethan's crooked, fake plant to shame. He wasn't sure that anything could spruce the place up, but he was willing to give it a shot if it meant he wouldn't lose Trina.

Monica even came bearing already framed photographs. She put a picture of Trina and Tootie playing tug-of-war with a shoelace in Ethan's room and a picture of Ethan wearing his tool belt and a flannel shirt in Trina's room. On the fireplace mantel, she put a picture of him and Trina riding the ski lift—looking like happy father and daughter adventurers, despite the fact that Trina had taken the lift right back down. There was also a picture of Trina and Gran doing a dance move in the Alvarezes' living room.

"Who took these?" he asked, absently scratching at the back of his neck. He certainly didn't remember posing for any of them.

"I found the first two on Gran's phone and got them developed. I took the one of Trina and Gran dancing, and Freckles didn't tell me how she came by the one of you guys on the slopes. It's a small town and I guess she has her connections."

He'd assumed that most people in town knew that Monica was helping him with Trina, but hope threaded through him at the realization that she wasn't keeping their relationship a secret. In fact, she was obviously enlisting the help of the locals in an effort to be a part of this support system Trina kept mentioning.

As Monica stood in his living room surveying her handiwork of throw pillows and knitted afghans and half-burned pillar candles, Ethan came up behind her. When he put his hands around her waist, she startled but she didn't pull away. She peeked behind them, probably to make sure Trina wasn't in the room, and then she leaned back against him. *Man, this felt right.* Lowering his lips to her neck, he asked, "What about a photo with you in it?"

She stiffened, but he didn't let her go far. Moving to the other side of her neck, he murmured, "Maybe I'll ask around over at the VFW and see if anyone got a shot of you in that short green dress. Wearing those sexy cowboy boots…"

She sighed as his fingers crept underneath her soft, blue sweater and danced along her warm skin as his palms made their way over her rib cage.

"When can I see you again?" he asked, his lips now just behind her ear. He felt her shudder, but the oven timer squawked and she practically jumped out of his arms.

As they utilized the polka-dot tablecloth she'd brought over, he sat across the dining table from her, eating a premade chicken potpie he'd picked up from the café and watching her try and pretend that she wasn't thinking about their next time together.

On Wednesday afternoon, despite Trina needing several reassurances from him in the morning that everything would be fine—as well as two bathroom passes while she was at school—the home visit went off without a hitch. The first thing Ethan did was offer up a prayer of thanks that nobody, especially his daughter, had seen through his false bravado. The second thing he did was send Monica a text message to celebrate the caseworker's recommendation that Trina stay with him.

She was at Legacy Village and replied with a picture of Gran painting a very unfortunate likeness of Elvis during the watercolor class. My grandmother thinks you look like him.

Ethan chuckled to himself before typing a response. I'll take it. You can give it to me tomorrow night when we meet at Patrelli's to celebrate.

She met them for dinner on Thursday night and, when Trina went into the back room of the restaurant to play arcade games, Ethan reached across the table and took Monica's hand. "When are we going to see each other again?"

"I'm seeing you right now," she said, but her eyes dropped to his lips and all of his blood dropped to his lower parts.

"You know what I mean."

"Maybe this weekend?" Monica's voice came out in a shy whisper and Ethan doubted he could wait that long.

Friday morning, he dropped off Trina at school and when Monica arrived to the library nearly an hour before it opened, he was waiting in the parking lot with a stack of books Trina had checked out and already read.

"I hope you're not here to pick up that new Navy SEAL book that came out on Tuesday," Monica said as she exited her car. "Mr. Simon beat you to it and checked it out yesterday."

"Mr. Simon can keep it," he replied, trying to keep his lips from sneering in disgust. An embedded journalist had written a fictionalized account of Ethan's unit and, from what he'd heard from Luke, the story contained a rather heroic retelling of the night Boscoe had died. "I already lived the nonfiction version and it's something I'd like to forget."

He felt the weight of her gaze as she studied him. "So that was you in the book? The one who single-handedly fought off all those insurgents in the middle of a crowded marketplace? And then carried your partner's body up to the roof and jumped across several buildings to make it to the medic's helicopter?"

"Well, I remember there being a lot more to the story than that." Specifically, the part about how he'd been the one to inadvertently lead his partner into the ambush in the first place. Monica tilted her head, her eyes full of comfort and a willingness to listen. However, Ethan didn't get many moments alone with the woman and he didn't want to waste the current one by talking about his past mistakes. He held up the stack of Trina's books. "Anyway, I'm actually just bringing these back."

"You know you can use the book return." Monica pointed to the metal box with a drop slot. "You didn't need to wait for me to get here."

"Maybe I just wanted to get you alone."

She looked at her watch, then looked at him, then looked at the empty parking lot. "I have to open the library in forty-five minutes."

"All I need is thirty," he replied with a hopeful lift of his forehead.

Inside the closet-sized storage room behind the circulation desk, Ethan hoisted Monica onto a metal book trolley and then proceeded to prove that he only needed half that amount of time.

She sighed contentedly when he withdrew from her and he couldn't help but watch her flushed chest rise and fall with each breath afterward.

He was already looking forward to the next time he could see her. "Someday, we'll have to actually make it to a bedroom."

"Well, we certainly shouldn't make a habit of doing it here." She felt around the shelf beside her until her hand landed on her discarded glasses. When she got them on, he helped her down to her feet before she tugged her skirt back over her hips.

"I'd suggest going to my job site next time, but starting Monday, Kane and I are building a new fish cleaning station near the Lake Rush boat launch."

"Is the city paying for that? Because the council postponed their vote on my request to expand our audiobook collection."

"Don't worry. Nobody is paying for it." He held up his palms. She lifted an eyebrow and he continued, "I've been known to give back to the community on occasion."

"You're racking up quite the list of good deeds, Ethan Renault." Monica folded her arms in front of her. "In fact, I've seen your name on the visitor log over at Legacy Village every day this week."

"Well, the day shift nurse said I'm the only one who can get your gran to slow down long enough between activities to drink a meal replacement shake."

Monica rubbed at the crease between her brows.

"What's wrong? Are you worried about your grandmother?"

"Well, that. And the fact that I'm not so sure we should be crossing all these boundaries and becoming so involved in each other's lives."

Ethan buttoned up the front of his jeans. "Don't you think it's a little too late for that, Mon?"

* * *

Nicole was heading quickly in her direction when Monica finally arrived at the check-in desk at Legacy Village later that afternoon. On the phone, the nurse had explained that they had things under control, but wanted to keep Monica informed about this latest episode.

The whole drive down there, though, she'd been beating herself up over the fact that she couldn't rush to Gran's aid sooner. But at least her grandmother was being taken care of by professionals and wasn't home alone or wreaking havoc on the local businesses on Snowflake Boulevard. By the time she'd pulled into the parking lot, Monica wasn't any closer to deciding if a memory care center was the right choice or not.

"Sorry I couldn't get here sooner," Monica said, already dreading the worst. "We had our teen reading challenge meeting and I couldn't close the library until four. Is she okay?"

"She's doing better now. Our doctor was making rounds and gave her a little sedative. She isn't asleep yet, but she's not crying anymore. Ethan is in her room with her."

"Ethan's here?" Monica asked, slapping the visitor sticker on her chest as she strode down the hall with Nicole on her heels.

"I called him when you said you couldn't be here right away. Mrs. Alvarez kept asking for *mijo* and I've heard her call him that before."

Trina was sitting in one of the overstuffed chairs in the hallway alcove near Gran's room, her headphones in her ears and her backpack at her feet. It must've been a really bad episode if Ethan had come straight from the school and was making his daughter wait outside.

When Monica slipped inside the room, she saw Ethan in a chair near Gran's bed. The older woman was fully dressed, but under the covers and holding Ethan's hand.

"Gran?" Monica whispered, brushing the silver hair off her grandmother's forehead. Her paper-thin eyelids fluttered open.

"There you are, Bettina. Look who came to stay at the hotel. My *mijo*." Gran's bony fingers squeezed against Ethan's hand and she mumbled something in Spanish that sounded like a recited prayer.

"That was nice of you to come keep her company, Ethan," Monica said.

"It's not Ethan," Gran replied, her words forceful yet somewhat slurred. "It's Fidel. My Fidel. He's finally home."

Ethan smiled when Gran patted his cheek but, when the older woman closed her eyes again, he got Monica's attention and mouthed the words, "Who's Fidel?"

"My dad." Monica hadn't replied out loud either, but just feeling the answer against her lips pierced her heart. She sat on the edge of the bed and her grandmother looked up. "How are you feeling, Gran?"

"Never been better." Gran's smile was faint, but genuine. "I have my son home and we're finally going to be a family. Look at all those muscles he built up while he was at the academy."

What academy? A prickling of unease spread through Monica as her grandmother kept talking.

"Don't I have the best son in the world, Bettina? He's always taken such good care of me."

Monica's jaw locked into place to keep her from responding the way she wanted to. She knew that she wasn't supposed to correct someone who was confused by Alzheimer's as long as their confusion wasn't harming them. But Gran's current bout with mistaken identity was bringing back some pretty painful memories for Monica. Especially since her deceased, deadbeat father was now getting unfair credit and glowing accolades when it was *she* who'd put her life on hold to take care of her grandmother.

"My *mijo* is going to take such good care of his baby girl, too," Gran continued to no one in particular, now. "As soon as he puts all those bad guys away, he will come home and take care of us. I know it."

Gran mumbled something else before her eyes drifted closed and remained that way for a few minutes, suggesting the sedative had finally taken full effect.

"Nicole said that a lot of people with dementia or Alzheimer's can get pretty anxious around this time of day." Ethan's voice was soft and low, probably because he didn't want to wake Gran again and have her confuse him for her low-life son. "The nurses called it 'sundowners' because it comes on when the sun goes down. It's not exactly my best time of the day either."

She knew he was trying to help, trying to make Monica feel better, but his compassion and understanding were only driving that wedge of unease in deeper. Between her guilt for leaving her grandmother at a nursing home and her sudden resentment that Gran wasn't even aware of how hard Monica was trying to do her best, she was dealing with too many emotions to add an ill-advised attraction to a single father to the mix.

Her grandmother let out a snore and Ethan gently extracted his hand and stood up. "The doctor said once the sedative took effect, she'd probably be out for the night. I've got to go get Trina some dinner. You wanna come with?"

"No, I'm not very hungry. What do you think she meant when she said you got back from the academy?"

Ethan lifted his shoulders. "Did your dad go to some sort of prep school?"

"Nope. He was a local kid, as far as I know," she replied, thinking of the boxes in the attic where Gran had stored her father's old things. Obviously, her grandmother had been beyond confused and clearly hadn't known what she'd been talking about. Although. This was different. Most of her episodes were usually centered around something she wanted or something that had actually happened in her past. Gran had never completely made something up out of the blue before.

"Okay, so maybe we can still get together this weekend?" Ethan asked.

"Sure," she said absently, as she focused on Gran's slurred words. Dealing with her grandmother's episodes had become such a part of Monica's routine, it was hard not to worry that the disease had become contagious. If her own mind was now slipping, as well.

Ethan studied Monica for a few more moments before placing a light kiss on her lips and walking out the door. She moved to the chair he'd vacated, but after about five minutes, when it became clear that Gran wasn't going to wake up and answer her questions anytime soon, Monica headed out to the parking lot and drove straight home.

Determination fueling her.

Chapter Fourteen

The return trip up the mountain was a complete blur, as though Monica's hands and feet were operating on autopilot, while her mind spun out of control. Letting herself in the house, she dropped her purse at the door and grabbed a package of Oreos from the kitchen before heading up to the attic.

Two hours later, Monica was sore from sitting cross-legged on the uneven wooden slats. Her eyes hurt from the lack of decent lighting and her brain was even more confused than when she'd started this pointless task.

The boxes contained all the same pictures and trophies and high school yearbooks she'd seen before. Her dad had been an all-star in both track and baseball at Sugar Falls High School, and had graduated as salutatorian. He'd gotten a scholarship to the University of Idaho, which was where he'd met her mom. There were a couple of wedding photos, but that was where all the clues ended. So how did her father fall into such a bad crowd?

The memories she had of him were few and far between, but most of them involved him leaving for long periods of time and then returning later with a book and a tight squeeze, teasing her about how big she was getting. She remembered looking forward to those visits, but she also recalled Fidel Alvarez's sudden presence having the opposite effect on his wife. And how could Monica enjoy seeing her dad when her mom was so clearly miserable?

One time, he'd showed up on a motorcycle, stayed a night or two and then fought with her mother before leaving in the middle of the night. When Monica was six, she'd gone on a long road trip with just her and her mom. She couldn't think of the name of the prison, but she remembered being fascinated by all the tattoos covering his arms when they sat across from him in the visiting area. She also recalled him being upset with her mother for bringing Monica.

Her mom had said that her dad would rather live with a bunch of druggies and crooks than be with his own family. That's when she'd made Monica promise never to fall in love with the same type of guy—a guy who didn't put his family first.

After her mother died, Monica made a promise to herself to not even give the man who'd fathered her a second thought. There'd been a couple of times in high school when she'd see his name on one of the plaques in the trophy case and she'd thought about doing some online research to find out more about him. After all, he obviously had a criminal record and she might be genetically predisposed and at risk for heading down the same unfortunate path.

Then she'd come to her senses and convinced herself that any answers she might uncover would only depress her. Instead, she'd buckled down on her studies and wouldn't attend so much as a school dance, let alone a party, just to prove that she was nothing like him.

The sound of a lawn mower rumbled to life and Monica looked at the time on her cell phone. It was almost seven o'clock on a Friday evening, which meant that Mr. Simon must be getting a late start on his yard maintenance. Either that or he needed a ploy to spy on poor Mrs. Fitzroy's delivery driver.

Wait. Mr. Simon had lived next door to Gran since before Monica was born. Maybe he could give her some insight about the man who'd abandoned her. Her legs revolted when she rose to her feet, but her circulation was back to normal by the time she got outside and waved down her neighbor.

"What can I do for you, Monica?" Mr. Simon had shut off his lawn mower, but he was blatantly staring at the big brown truck now driving away. His eyes narrowed behind his wire-rimmed glasses. "Awful late in the day to deliver a package."

"Mr. Simon, do you remember my father?"

"Fidel? Of course. Who wouldn't remember him?"

His daughter, Monica thought. "Gran's been asking about him a lot. Can you tell me anything?"

"Boy, that guy could run. Won the eight hundred meter at state two years in a row. He was a couple of years behind me at high school, but he was smarter than anyone I ever hung around. And he loved pickles."

"No, I know all about when he was young." Except the pickles part, which finally explained Gran's surplus in the pantry. She was hoping her son would be coming home to eat them. "But what can you tell me about him after he got married?"

Mr. Simon let out a low whistle.

Monica twisted her lower lip between her teeth. "Tell me."

"Well, I hate to say it, but he really never should've married your mom. Not with his lifestyle."

Monica seized on the opening she needed. "What about his lifestyle?"

"Come to think of it, that boyfriend of yours reminds me of Fidel in a lot of ways." Mr. Simon tapped his chin and Monica felt every muscle inside of her coil at the comparison. Ethan most definitely was not her boyfriend, but she wasn't going to argue the small details when she needed to understand the bigger picture.

"Why? Is it because of his…" She had almost said *addiction*, but at the last second caught herself. Talking about Ethan's alcoholism would've been a violation of his trust. "Lifestyle?"

"Fidel was one of those macho hero types. Always good at sports and always wanting to save the world. He was this happy-go-lucky guy who was the life of the party and could fit in with anyone. Nobody was surprised when he joined the DEA after college. But when he started taking on those undercover assignments, your mom was not having it. And who could blame her?"

"DEA? You mean Drug Enforcement Administration?" Maybe Mr. Simon had read a few too many true crime books. "Are you sure?"

"You mean your grandma didn't tell you?"

Monica shook her head. Nobody had told her. "I thought he was on the other side of the law, so to speak. My mom took me to visit him in prison before she died.

He got so mad at her and wouldn't even look at me, let alone hug me."

"Yep, your gran told me about that. That was back before we had a local police force. I had to organize the neighborhood watch so we could take turns keeping an eye out to make sure none of his associates came looking for you."

"What do you mean his *associates*?"

"The kind he was infiltrating. Fidel had gone so deep undercover, even the prison guards didn't know he was a special agent. Your mom drove you down to Florence, Colorado, to show him that his work was causing him to miss out on your childhood."

"They fought in the visiting area," Monica said softly. "He yelled at her."

"It was actually a pretty reckless thing for your mom to do. Fidel was investigating a major drug ring that ended up taking down a dozen or so guards, four supervisors and the assistant warden. By bringing you to that prison, she was painting a target on both of your backs and providing his enemies with the perfect means to exact their revenge. Even when the case was over and he was done testifying, he still stayed away just to make sure you were safe. He died shortly after that in a routine drug bust that went bad. At least, that's what they told your grandmother."

"Is that why I wasn't allowed to go to his funeral?"

"That would be my guess. He was Lydia's only son and she was already devastated. You were all she had left after that." Mr. Simon jabbed a finger in the air. "Actually, I have some pictures of him and you when you were a baby. The neighborhood threw a big party when he came home from the academy. Things were a little tense around here after he died so your gran asked me to hold onto some of his awards and the newspaper articles just in case any of those bad dudes he put away came looking for you. There's a *Law and Order* marathon on tonight, but I can look for them tomorrow and bring them over."

Monica thanked her neighbor and returned to the house in a daze. Gran hadn't avoided talking about her dad because she was too sad. She'd done it to keep Monica safe. Now that she thought about it, even her mother had never come out and called Fidel a drug addict. But they'd never filled in any of the blanks either, and Monica had been left to think the worst.

The pieces of a puzzle she hadn't known existed began clicking into place. Her father showing up late for her birthday party and her mom yelling at him for missing it. Her father disappearing for stretches of time and then reappearing out of the blue with disheveled hair and an overgrown beard that made her mom complain there was no way she was going to take family pictures with him until he "cleaned up his act."

Her entire childhood, she'd thought her father was some lowlife, some criminal. That his addiction had come before anything else. Apparently, his addiction hadn't been to drugs, but to his career.

She saw a missed text from Ethan, but Monica's head was still swimming and she didn't want to think about anything but how wrong she'd been about everything in her life up until now.

The entire weekend went by and Ethan didn't hear from Monica. He knew she'd been stressed out about that incident at Legacy Village the previous Friday, so he hadn't wanted to push her.

On Monday afternoon, he was going to send her a

text asking her whether he should make alternate arrangements for Trina, but when his daughter came home from school, she said Kayla Patrelli invited her to Bring a Friend night at the Snowflake Dance Academy. He'd been hoping she would express some sort of interest in an extracurricular activity that involved actually being active.

Plus, maybe Monica was right. They'd been getting too involved in each other's lives lately.

On Tuesday afternoon, when he brought Trina to tutoring, Monica kept her distance. However, several times he caught her watching him, her expression leery as if he had suddenly grown two heads.

"Why are you looking at me like that?" he asked her when he passed by the checkout desk.

"Like what?" Monica kept her eyes averted, as though she was now suddenly too busy to notice him standing right in front of her. She was opening book covers and scanning barcodes and stacking them on the same metal trolley where he'd made love to her a few mornings ago.

"You haven't returned any of my texts. Did something happen on Friday after I left Legacy Village?"

Her hands stilled over a cellophane-covered copy of *The Great Gatsby*. When her eyes finally rose to his, they were somewhat vacant behind the lenses of her glasses. "I found out that my father wasn't who I thought he was. My grandmother never told me the truth. And now she's at the point where she can hardly remember what the truth is anymore."

"Mon, she's still your family even if you're not related by blood." Ethan leaned his elbows on the polished wood counter separating them. "When Trina first showed up, I thought about getting DNA tests. But even if I didn't already believe deep down that she was mine, I would've wanted her anyway. I'm sure your grandmother feels the same about you."

The creased V appeared above her nose before she shoved her glasses back into place. "No, I'm not talking about biologically. I mean my dad wasn't some drug dealing criminal. He was actually an undercover DEA agent."

"Oh yeah. I read that he took down one of the biggest drug operations in the federal prison system."

Monica's head drew back. "How did you know that?"

"I did an internet search. I wanted to know more about the guy your gran was mistaking me for in case I needed to get her settled down again."

"Why have you been so good to her?" Monica asked. "You have all of your own issues with your meetings and your job and becoming a full-time single dad overnight. You've already got me to sleep with you. So why are you still hanging around and being nice to Gran?"

"Because I want to do more than just sleep with you, Monica."

"Why?" she asked, her neck stretching back as she looked up at him. He realized the mistrust he'd thought she'd overcome was back in full force. "What does an adrenaline junkie like you see in a bookworm like me?"

"Because you're smart and you're serious and you're stable."

"Stable? Wow. You really know how to get a girl's pulse racing." She turned to look at the same boy who had been asking her for the frog book a couple of weeks ago, and was now on his tippy-toes, using the second shelf of the medical section as a stepladder. "Do you need me to help you find something, Choogie?"

With a final stretch, the boy toppled over a hefty volume on human anatomy. "Nope, Miz Monica. I got it."

Choogie kept the cover turned toward his chest as he

ran-walked to a back table where the Gregson twins were eagerly awaiting them. Monica groaned under her breath. "Last week, they found a stash of *National Geographic* magazines in the Friends of the Library donation pile. I'm going to have to go check on them before they get to the chapter on reproductive parts."

"Then I'll make this quick." Ethan remembered what it was like to be curious at that age and wanted to tell the boys that no book was going to make the opposite sex any less mysterious. Taking a fortifying breath, he continued. "I moved around a lot when I was a kid. Then, when I was in the Navy, I never slept in the same bed longer than six months at a time. Usually way less than that. So when I say stable, I mean I like the fact that you were born and raised here and that you're established in the community and not going anywhere. I want to settle down, Mon. I want to belong somewhere and I want my daughter to have what I never experienced."

"Most of the single women who live in Sugar Falls are just as stable," Monica challenged.

"But it's calm when I'm with you. More importantly, *I'm* calm when I'm with you. Like I don't need to jump out of a plane or dive off a cliff or race down a mountain when you're around. I'm not saying I won't do those things in the future. But when we're together, I'm not looking for anything else to stir my blood. I liked you before Trina ever showed up, but then I saw you with her and I was an absolute goner. You know what to do for her before I can even figure out the right question to ask. She needs you almost as much as I do."

"Ethan, I don't think I can be needed by anyone else right now. Between my jobs and Gran, I'm barely keeping my head above water."

"So then why don't you depend on someone else for a change?" he asked.

"Like you?" She rolled her eyes and his chest filled with disappointment. "You're renting a furnished apartment by the month and you haven't even unpacked those boxes in your bedroom yet. You said that you wanted stability. Well, so do I."

Monica hadn't even tried to ease the blow before walking away to retrieve the book Choogie and the Gregson twins were now hovering over. She'd left Ethan standing there to contemplate the absolute reality of her harsh words.

He needed her, but he had absolutely nothing that she needed.

On Wednesday morning, Ethan was supposed to run electrical wiring to Freckles's backyard gazebo for her new hot tub. Kane was Freckles's nephew by marriage and, when the café owner told him and Ethan about some of the best hot tub parties she'd attended in the seventies, Kane had picked up his tool bag and told Ethan, "You're on your own."

So when the dark clouds finally opened up to deliver the spring showers the weather channel had predicted, Ethan rolled up the conduit and wires and decided not to get electrocuted that day. There was an AA meeting he could attend at Shadowview at ten, but when Ethan went home to change into some dry clothes, he saw Tootie sitting on top of the cardboard boxes, gnawing at one of the corners.

Well, he thought, pushing up his sleeves, if he wanted Monica to think he was stable, maybe he should take her advice and finally unpack these boxes once and for all.

The first one was easy. Mostly papers and files. He scanned over his performance ratings from the Navy and his father's last banking statement that the attorney had sent him after his old man had passed away. Between his small inheritance from his dad and all the extra deployment pay he'd stashed away, there was no reason why he couldn't buy one of the older Victorian homes over on Pinecone Court and fix it up for him and Trina. That would definitely demonstrate to him and everyone else that he was just as stable as the next person.

The second box had some photos and several plaques and awards from his days on the team. Maybe if he found a place with a den or an office conversion, he could hang some of these on the wall.

When he got to the third box, though, Ethan wanted to close it back up as soon as he opened it. Standing up, he went to the kitchen to make another cup of coffee. Tootie meowed, as she always did anytime someone got close to the refrigerator. "The vet said no more snacks. If I have to become stable, then your digestive tract needs to become stable, as well."

He downed half the cup before carrying it back into his bedroom and facing the box that contained some of Damon Boscoe's personal effects. The ones he was supposed to send to his buddy's family more than two years ago. The faded T-shirt advertising the Recovery Tour he'd gotten when he and Ethan snuck off base to go to an Eminem concert. The sweat-stained bandana printed with the Texas flag that Boscoe always wore under his helmet. The tied stack of letters from his mom that smelled like vanilla cookies. He shifted through more pictures and then his eyes landed on it. Boscoe's lucky shell he'd found in the sand after barely passing their combat dive phase. It still had his friend's blood on it from the night Ethan had held him in his arms as the desert sky lit up with gunfire rounds and missiles while they'd waited for backup to arrive.

Losing a team member in battle was something Ethan had been through before. But with Boscoe it had been different. Both of them were from Texas, they'd ridden together on the same bus to recruit training and they'd been stationed to the same destroyer after graduation. They'd even received their letters welcoming them to BUD/S training on the same day. Boscoe had been the only brother he'd ever known.

And Ethan had killed him.

Or at least, he hadn't saved him.

After a full investigation, the inquiry board determined that Ethan hadn't been at fault for the attack that had taken Boscoe's life. But Ethan hadn't been at his best either. He'd polished off a bottle of vodka the night before, after celebrating the capture of one of the top ranking terrorists in the area. His head was still fuzzy and his entire body was hungover when the base commander had ordered them to follow up on a tip about a possible retaliation attack. If Ethan had been thinking clearly, he never would've walked into that marketplace without suspecting a trap.

Ethan's responses had been slower and his best friend had paid the price. He'd like to say that he got sober the very next day. But it wasn't until Luke Gregson was standing on the tarmac beside him back in the States as they lowered Boscoe's casket from the plane. Luke told Ethan about his first wife dying in a DUI and how he'd always blamed himself for not speaking up sooner and getting a loved one the help they needed. Luke had then handed him a flyer listing all the local AA meetings near the Coronado base.

Ethan now dug in the cardboard box again and picked up the piece of paper that Luke had given him that day. It was crumpled and stained with pizza sauce and had been covering half a bottle of Jim Beam.

That's right, the memory slammed into Ethan. He'd

been drinking when he'd originally packed this box. He'd gone to refill his cup with ice, and saw the list of AA meetings he'd thrown in the trash. He'd been completely sloshed when he'd called the number on the flyer and didn't remember taping the box closed that night.

Now, as he held the glass neck of the bottle in his hand, he realized that day eighteen months ago was the first time Ethan hadn't finished a bottle. So much had changed since that night and he would like to think he was strong enough in his recovery to keep the half-empty bottle as some sort of trophy. Some sort of reminder that he'd stopped mid-drink and never needed a drop of booze again.

But then he looked outside his bedroom door, at the floral quilt covering his daughter's bed, and he knew that nothing would be worth losing her. He wasn't even going to risk the possibility of temptation. Standing up, he didn't bother taking the time to walk all the way to the kitchen sink. Instead, he went straight to the bathroom and began pouring the contents down the toilet.

Unfortunately, he'd left the door open too long and Tootie decided it was the perfect time to attack the unattended toilet paper roll. The kitten missed her target, though, and knocked into Ethan, causing him to splash a fair amount of bourbon all over the front of his clean T-shirt.

He was about to change into another, but his cell phone vibrated in his pocket.

"Hi, Dad." Trina's voice echoed off the acoustics of what must've been the girls' bathroom.

"Trina, what's wrong? Why aren't you in class?"

"Can you come to the school? I really need you."

"I'll be there in five minutes," Ethan said, already halfway down the steps outside before he disconnected.

Chapter Fifteen

When Monica arrived in the girls' bathroom at Sugar Falls Elementary, Ethan was already there and sitting on the counter between two sinks, apparently not caring that a gaggle of schoolgirls could walk in at any second.

And he smelled like a distillery. Had he been drinking? Disappointment made her legs turn to lead as she walked closer to the sinks, but she'd deal with him later.

"Where's Trina?" Monica asked. "What happened?"

Ethan used his thumb to gesture toward one of the closed stall doors and that was when she noticed his daughter's shoes underneath.

Had Ethan shown up drunk at the school and made some sort of scene?

The lock slid open and Trina emerged with her phone in her hands. The girl wasn't looking down or hiding her face, though. In fact, she didn't appear to be upset at all.

"I got your text that you were here, honey," Monica told the girl. "Why are you hiding in the bathroom?"

"It's Wednesday," Trina said, as though that explained everything.

"Are you worried about your math test?" Ethan asked his daughter, and Monica realized he was just as clueless as to why Trina had resorted to hiding out in the bathroom. Again. "I thought that was tomorrow."

Monica glared at Ethan and mouthed, *Are you drunk?*

He frowned at her and gave a quick shake of his head before hopping off the counter. Hmm, he appeared steady enough on his feet.

She would've assessed his sobriety more, however, Trina began speaking again. "No. I'm not worried about my math test. I mean, I will be tomorrow, but I figured the sooner I got you guys together the better."

"Okay, so it's Wednesday and you've got us both here, Trina. She wouldn't tell me what was going on until you arrived," Ethan told Monica then turned back to his daughter. "Is everything okay?"

"No, it's not." Trina planted her hands on her hips. "Both of you guys have told me that you want to do what's best for me, right?"

"Definitely," Monica replied at the same time Ethan said, "Of course."

She and Ethan were now standing side by side and Trina's brows were lifted in challenge as she faced them. "Well, it's best for me if you guys are dating and making each other happy."

Ethan lifted his eyes to the ceiling and made a choking noise that suspiciously sounded like a smothered chuckle. Monica opened her mouth to protest, but Trina held up her palms. "I know you two haven't been talking. Dad, you were looking at your cell phone every five minutes last weekend waiting to hear from her. And, Monica, when we visited Gran on Sunday, she told me that you were crazy about my dad and it would be up to me to get you back together."

"Honey, you can't listen to what Gran says half the time—" Monica started, but Trina cut her off by pointing her little eleven-year-old finger right at them.

"Gran told me that was exactly what you'd say. When I saw you staring at my dad in the library yesterday I knew she was right."

Ethan's nose made a hissing sound as he drew in a deep breath. "So you decided the best way to get us together was to call both of us and tell us that it was an emergency and we needed to meet you in the girls' room in the middle of the school day?"

"I never said it was an emergency. But it's Wednesday and my tutoring session tomorrow got canceled so I knew that I needed to do something quick or else you guys wouldn't see each other until next Monday again. It worked when Gran had you both show up together, so I figured it would work for me."

"It's more complicated than just getting us alone to talk." Monica looked at Ethan. "Back me up here anytime."

Ethan merely shrugged, the fabric of his shirt releasing its boozy odor in the air. "No harm ever came from talking."

"Okay, so you guys have about twenty minutes until the lunch bell rings and everyone heads this way." Trina put her cell phone in the back pocket of her jeans. "I have to go back to class right now, but I'll be in the cafeteria later if you need my advice."

Advice for what? Monica thought. But as the door closed behind the girl, Monica wanted to call out and ask her to come back so she wouldn't have to face Ethan alone.

"So what do you want to discuss first?" he asked, leaning a hip against the bathroom counter as though he was ready to settle in for the long haul.

A little girl wearing pigtails and a laminated hall pass around her neck shoved through the door and paused. She looked back and forth between Ethan and Monica before glancing up at the sign on the door that clearly read Girls.

"We were just leaving," Ethan told the child as he cupped Monica's elbow and steered her into the hall. She thought she'd gotten another reprieve, but then he added, "We can finish our discussion outside."

When they got out to the parking lot, it was still drizzling and Ethan watched Monica clean the splatters off her glasses. "It's really coming down, huh?"

"It's barely a mist," he pointed out. "Or are you so desperate to avoid me, you're going to pretend we're in a category four hurricane?"

"I haven't been avoiding you." She wrapped her arms around her waist and stared at the empty flagpole behind him.

"Okay, well I see we're not going to get anywhere by actually talking about what's going on." Ethan's lower lip curved into a frown as he nodded. "Let me know when you're ready to have a conversation."

He pulled the keys out of his pocket and Monica made a sputtering sound. "Are you sure you should be driving in your condition?"

"In what condition?" Ethan had seen the way she'd

looked at him in disgust earlier when she'd walked inside the bathroom and took her first whiff of him. But he wanted to hear her say it out loud. She didn't trust him.

"Oh come on, Ethan. You smell like you've been doing shots all morning."

"No, I smell like I was dumping a bottle of bourbon down the toilet and a kitten tried to attack the toilet paper roll and knocked the contents all over me."

"Why did you have a bottle of bourbon in the bathroom?"

"I found it when I was finally going through those boxes in an effort to get 'stable' for you." Oh great. He'd just used air quotes. There was no pretending that he wasn't completely off his rocker now. "But then I got a call from Trina and I practically flew over here."

"Oh."

"Oh?" Ethan moved both of his hands on his hips. "That's all I get is an 'oh'?"

"I'm sorry for thinking you had a relapse." Her curls were getting tighter in the rain and she shoved a hand through them.

"I'm not going to pretend that it doesn't hurt to know that you doubt me, Monica. And I'm not going to pretend that there's no chance I'll ever have a relapse. I'm a work in progress, okay? But at least I'm trying to put myself out there."

"I'm having uncomplicated, mind-blowing, soul-reaching, earth-shattering sex with the most attractive man I've ever laid my eyes on," she said, and Ethan felt the edges of his mouth reverse course and turn up into a grin. So she thought their sex was mind-blowing, too? He would've followed up on that last part, but she wasn't done talking. "At least I thought it would be uncomplicated until all of my emotions got involved. Do you have any idea how outside of my comfort zone that is? You don't think I'm putting myself out there, too?"

Ethan had to tamp down the pride rising in his chest so he could keep her talking. "I think you're upset about your grandmother and you're dealing with all this new stuff about your dad. But I also think it's easier for you to hold me off at a distance."

"Don't you see that I *have* to keep you at a distance, Ethan? That I have to protect myself?"

"Protect yourself from what?"

"From falling in love with you!" she yelled in a very nonlibrarian way.

Ethan's lungs seized at her admission, and then his pulse sprang back to life so quickly, his heart felt as if it was blasting against his rib cage. "Why would you want to stop doing that?"

"What if you left?" she asked, her voice no longer as confident as when she'd been yelling.

"What if *you* did?" he countered.

"Why would I leave?"

"I don't know. Maybe for the same reasons you think I might. The past four weeks, you've been refusing to make any promises and commitments, yet that didn't stop me from falling absolutely completely crazy in love with you."

"But you're a risk-taker, Ethan. I'm not like you."

"Not when it comes to my emotions, I'm not. But I also know that I can't stay safe and let life pass me by."

"Are you saying that I'm letting life pass me by?"

"I believe it was your gran who said that."

"But you clearly agree with her," Monica accused.

"Listen. The other day, you asked me why I was attracted to you and I put it all out there, yet you *still* blew me off. My feelings weren't enough for you. *I* wasn't enough for you."

"Of course you're enough for me. You're more than I have ever wanted. But happily-ever-afters are only in books. We need more than just a connection. Than just a physical attraction."

"So you admit that you're attracted to me?" Ethan exhaled. "At least that's a start."

"I think we established that on my staircase and then again in the closet behind the circulation desk at the library." The dampness in the air coupled with the heat radiating from Monica's blushing cheeks made her glasses steam up.

"That's why you had sex with me." He carefully took her glasses off and used his dry T-shirt under his flannel to wipe them clean before setting them back on her nose. "But why did you help me so much with Trina? Why did you share so much of yourself with me?"

Monica took a deep breath, then shuddered. "Because you're strong and you're resilient and you don't give up. I love that when you're completely out of your element, you still do your best to get things right. I love the fact that you try to understand Trina and where she's coming from, rather than defend yourself or push her to see things your way. I love the fact that you go to visit a little old lady every day, even though she doesn't know who you are most of the time, and that you patiently wait for your daughter at shopping malls and public restrooms despite the fact that you'd rather be skydiving off a cliff somewhere. I love the fact that when I'm in your arms, your eyes don't look so empty anymore. And I love the fact that you completely proved me wrong about the kind of man you are."

He stepped to her and brushed her hair away from her cheek. "You're using the L-word an awful lot. Does that mean that you're rethinking that whole no-promises, no-commitments thing?"

"I was rethinking it before I ever said it." She put her hands on his shoulders and sighed. "I love you, Ethan Renault."

The words floated around him, a sense of peace settling over him. He wanted to kiss her but he also wanted to stare at her and memorize the exact way she was looking at him right that second.

"I love you, too, Monica Alvarez," he said, feeling the words all the way down to his bones. "I know that things in our lives are crazy and chaotic and between Trina and your gran, we don't know what the next day will bring. All I can do is love you through it."

Monica's hands linked behind his neck and she pulled his head toward hers. "And all I can do is love you back."

Epilogue

The morning of April 8 was sunny and bright. It was also exactly two months since Trina's actual birth date, but Ethan insisted he wasn't going to wait until the following year to celebrate his daughter. Monica and Trina hung decorations in the backyard while Ethan drove to Legacy Village to check Gran out for the day so she could attend the belated birthday party.

Trina had invited several kids from her class, but when word got out that Ethan was renting an inflatable obstacle course and a bungee jumping trampoline, everyone from the neighborhood wanted to come celebrate the eleven-year-old.

"*Mija*, this is exactly what this house needed," her grandmother said, transferring a sleeping Tootie to the crook of her arm as she took the cup of frozen lemonade Monica brought her. "Children and friends and music and laughter. But why didn't you ask me to cook the food?"

"Well, Ethan lives above Domino's Deli and Mr. Domino offered to do the catering. Plus, I wanted you to sit back and enjoy the party." Gran had been pretty with it since she'd arrived a couple of hours ago, but that didn't mean that Monica was going to let her guard down when it came to sudden episodes. "How're you feeling, Gran?"

"I'm about as good as you'd expect. Some days are better than others."

"Do you hate it at Legacy Village? You don't have to go back."

"Actually, I rather enjoy it. Even when I feel like my old self, I enjoy it. You were always a quiet thing and, after your dad died, I had to keep to myself more. But I like people. I like being social and helping the other residents at the home. No offense, *mija*, but living at the house was so boring. You were always gone at work and I couldn't drive or have any fun. It's better that I'm there."

"I miss you, though, Gran." Tears filled Monica's eyes and she hated that she sounded like a spoiled child. Especially since they were surrounded by so many people who'd come there for a party.

"You miss who I *was*," her grandmother replied. "So do I. Unfortunately, I can't be that person anymore."

"Okay. But the house is pretty quiet without you."

"Then do what you did today. Bring some life into it."

"You *are* my life, Gran."

"No, you need a *real* life. Invite Ethan and Trina to move in with you. They can even bring their little cat with them."

Monica felt the heat climb her neck. It'd only been a few weeks since she and Ethan had admitted that they loved each other. She didn't want to scare the guy off as soon as she got him. "I think Ethan and Trina are happy living at their apartment."

"Actually—" Ethan sat down on one of the rented folding chairs next to them on the deck "—Trina hates the apartment and thinks it's too plain. Even with the borrowed decorations. I've always loved the houses on this street, though. Especially this one. When I was doing work on the kitchen a few months ago, I kept envisioning a sunroom right over there off the nook."

"You know, I always wanted one of those." Gran's eyes brightened. "I would've used it for a dance studio, but you could probably also make it a reading room for Monica and Trina."

Ethan's eyes locked on Monica as he took a chug of his own cup of frozen lemonade. When he set the drink down, he revealed that sexy smirk above that even sexier chin dimple. "I'm willing to make anything that Monica and Trina want."

Trina ran up to the deck right at that second, and passed Gran a piece of chocolate birthday cake. "Did you convince them yet?"

"I'm working on it, *mija*." Gran stage-whispered to the girl.

"Convince us of what?" Monica narrowed her eyes.

"You know, since you're building things, I also always wanted my own gazebo. Right over there." Gran pointed to the spruce tree in the corner. "It doesn't have to be as big as the one in Town Square Park, but something big enough for…oh…let's say a wedding ceremony? Think you can build one of those wedding gazebos, Ethan?"

Monica felt the heat rushing up her face and scooted to the edge of her seat, facing her grandmother so she could tell her to stop making such crazy suggestions. But Ethan's voice interrupted her.

"One wedding gazebo coming up." When Monica turned back around, Ethan was down on his knee, holding out a small box.

Everyone in the backyard went completely silent. Except for a lycra-clad Freckles, who'd just been launched on the bungee jump and was shrieking with laughter. Monica's stomach boinged just as hard.

She looked down at the ring box and then back at his sapphire-blue eyes, no longer hollow, but full of laughter and love and hope. "Is that…? Are you…?"

"I love you, Monica Alvarez. And if you marry me and promise me a life of stability, I'll promise you a life of adventure."

All she could do was nod and Ethan didn't bother putting the ring on her finger because he was too busy lifting her into his arms, her cowboy boots coming off the ground.

A cheer rose from everyone in the backyard and Trina jumped up and down before extending her hand to Gran's and giving the older woman a high five.

Theirs wouldn't be the typical family, and Monica knew they'd have their share of ups and downs down the road. But there was nobody else she'd rather have by her side.

* * * * *

COMING NEXT MONTH FROM

H HARLEQUIN®

SPECIAL EDITION

Available March 19, 2019

#2683 GUARDING HIS FORTUNE
The Fortunes of Texas: The Lost Fortunes • by Stella Bagwell
Savannah Fortune is off-limits, and bodyguard Chaz Mendoza knows it. The grad student he's been hired to look after is smart, opinionated—and rich. What would she want with a regular guy like Chaz? Her family has made it clear he has no permanent place in her world. But Chaz refuses to settle for anything less...

#2684 THE LAWMAN'S ROMANCE LESSON
Forever, Texas • by Marie Ferrarella
When Shania Stewart tells Deputy Daniel Tallchief that he needs to lighten up with his wild younger sister, the handsome lawman doesn't know whether to ignore her or kiss her. But Shania knows. It's going to take a carefully crafted lesson plan to tutor this cowboy in love.

#2685 TO KEEP HER BABY
The Wyoming Multiples • by Melissa Senate
After Ginger O'Leary learns she's pregnant, it's time for a whole new Ginger. James Gallagher is happy to help, but after years of raising his siblings, becoming attached isn't in the plan. But neither is the way his heart soars every time he and Ginger match wits. What will it take for these two opposites to realize that they're made for each other?

#2686 AN UNEXPECTED PARTNERSHIP
by Teresa Southwick
Leo Wallace had been duped—hard—once before, so he refuses to take Tess's word when she says she's pregnant. Now she wants Leo's help to save her family business, too. Leo agrees to be the partner Tess needs. But it's going to take a paternity test to make him believe this baby is his. He just can't trust his heart again...no matter what it's saying.

#2687 THE NANNY CLAUSE
Furever Yours • by Karen Rose Smith
When Daniel Sutton's daughters rescue an abandoned calico, the hardworking attorney doesn't expect to be sharing his home with a litter of newborns! And animal shelter volunteer Emma Alvarez is transforming the lives of Daniel and his three girls. The first-time nanny is a natural with kids and pets. Will that extend to a single father ready to trust in love again?

#2688 HIS BABY BARGAIN
Texas Legends: The McCabes • by Cathy Gillen Thacker
Ex-soldier turned rancher Matt McCabe wants to help his recently widowed friend and veterinarian, Sara Anderson. She wants him to join her in training service dogs for veterans—oddly, he volunteers to take care of her adorable eight-month-old son, Charley, instead. This "favor" feels more like family every day...though their troubled pasts threaten a happy future.

HSECNM0319

Shania flushed as she raised her eyes toward Daniel. "I
don't usually babble like this."

Daniel found the pink hue that had suddenly risen to
her cheeks rather sweet. The next second, he realized that
he was staring. Daniel forced himself to look away. "I
hadn't noticed."

"Yes, you had," Shania contradicted. "But I think that
it's very nice of you to pretend that you hadn't." When
she heard Daniel laugh softly to himself, she asked him,
"What's so funny?" before she could think to stop herself.

"I'm not accustomed to hearing the word *nice* used to
describe me," he admitted.

Didn't the man have any close friends? Someone to
bolster him up when he was down on himself? "You're
kidding."

The lopsided smile answered her before he did. "Something else I'm not known for."

She pretended that he was a student and she did a quick assessment of the man before her. "You know you're being very hard on yourself."

"Not hard," he contradicted. "Just honest."

She had no intention of letting this slide. If he had been one of her students, she would have done what she could to raise his spirits—or maybe it was his self-esteem that needed help.

"Well, I think you're nice—and you do have a sense of humor."

"If you say so," Daniel replied, not about to dispute the matter. He had a feeling that arguing with Shania would be pointless. "But just so you know, I'm not about to chuck my career and become a stand-up comedian."

She grinned at his words. "See, I told you that you had a sense of humor," she declared happily.

Don't miss
The Lawman's Romance Lesson *by Marie Ferrarella,*
available April 2019 wherever
Harlequin® *Special Edition books and ebooks are sold.*

www.Harlequin.com

They'd both just turned back to their work when a familiar loud, croaking sound cut the silence.

The twins shrieked and ran from where they'd been playing into the little cabin's yard and slammed into Anna, their faces frightened.

"What was that?" Anna sounded alarmed, too, kneeling to hold and comfort both girls.

"Nothing to be afraid of," Sean said, trying to hold back laughter. "It's just egrets. Type of water bird." He located the source of the sound, then went over to the trio, knelt beside them, and pointed through the trees and growth.

When the girls saw the stately white birds, they gasped.

"They're so pretty!" Anna said.

"Pretty?" Sean chuckled. "Nobody from around here would get excited about an egret, nor think it's especially pretty." But as he watched another one land beside the first, white wings spread wide as it skidded into the shallow water, he realized that there was beauty there. He just hadn't noticed it before.

That was what kids did for you: made you see the world through their fresh, innocent eyes. A fist of longing clutched inside his chest.

The twins were tugging at Anna's shirt now, trying to get her to take them over toward the birds. "You may go look as long as you can see me," she said, "but take careful steps by the water." She took the bolder twin's face in her hands. "The water's not deep, but I still don't want you to wade in. Do you understand?"

Both little girls nodded vigorously.

They ran off and she watched for a few seconds, then turned back to her work with a barely audible sigh.

"Go take a look with them," he urged her. "It's not every day kids see an egret for the first time."

"You're sure?"

"Go on." He watched her run like a kid over to her girls. And then he couldn't resist walking a few steps closer and watching them, shielded by the trees and brush.

The twins were so excited that they weren't remembering to be quiet. "It caught a *fish*!" the one was crowing, pointing at the bird, which, indeed, held a squirming fish in its mouth.

"That one's neck is like an S!" The quieter twin squatted down, rapt.

Anna eased down onto the sandy beach, obviously unworried about her or the girls getting wet or dirty, laughing and talking to them and sharing their excitement.

The sight of it gave him a melancholy twinge. His own mom had been a nature lover. She'd taken him and his brothers fishing, visited a nature reserve a few times, back in Alabama where they'd lived before coming here.

Oh, if things were different, he'd run with this, see where it led...

Don't miss
Lee Tobin McClain's Low Country Hero,
available March 2019 from HQN Books!

www.Harlequin.com